CAPTURED!

The warrior did not fire. Instead, barreling in on his large roan, he deliberately rammed his mount broadside into Davy's. The collision jolted the sorrel sideways. It tripped, tottered, nearly went down, and it was all Davy could do to stay in the saddle. Somehow he accomplished it. He heard a war whoop and raised his head just as the surly warrior closed in swinging a large knife. Its bone hilt connected with Davy's temple.

The world spun wildly. Davy struggled to stay conscious, flapping his legs to spur the sorrel out of there. His rifle began to slip from his fingers and he tightened his grip to keep from dropping it. When a second blow caught him on the forehead, agony speared through him clear down to his toes.

A black cloud swallowed Davy like the big fish did Jonah. He was dimly aware of falling, of hitting the ground on his left side.

After that he knew nothing.

The *Davy Crockett* Series:
#1: HOMECOMING

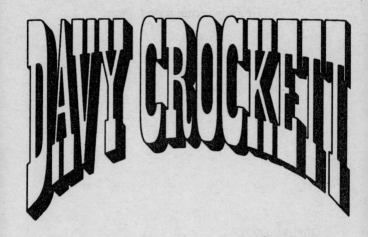

DAVY CROCKETT

SIOUX SLAUGHTER

David Thompson

LEISURE BOOKS   NEW YORK CITY

To Judy, Joshua and Shane

A LEISURE BOOK®

January 1997

Published by

Dorchester Publishing Co., Inc.
276 Fifth Avenue
New York, NY 10001

Printed in the United States of America.

SIOUX SLAUGHTER

David Thompson

Chapter One

"Have you ever seen so much grass in all your born days?" Davy Crockett asked in an awed tone. Before him stretched an unending sea of it. Even when he rose in the stirrups and placed a hand across his brow to shield his eyes from the glare of the sun, all he saw was grass, grass, and more grass.

"No, I reckon not," Flavius Harris answered glumly. He did not share his friend's excitement about the vast prairie. All he cared about was ending their gallivant and heading back to Tennessee.

"It's just like Lewis and Clark said it was," Davy marveled, kneeing his sorrel onward. For years he'd heard tales of the sprawling, mysterious plains. Now, to actually see the gently waving ocean of grass with his own eyes filled him with joy beyond words. "One day we can brag to our grandkids that we were here."

"If we live that long," Flavius grumbled. In his

7

view they were tempting fate by straying so far from home. He thought of his wife and how much he missed her, in particular the wonderful meals she made. What he wouldn't give for five or six helpings of her delicious chicken stew with dumplings! Or a dozen eggs with half a pound of bacon. Just dreaming about it made him giddy.

Sighing, Davy turned to regard his portly friend. Ever since they had parted company with the Ojibwas, Flavius had grown more and more moody. "Consarn it all," he said. "What will it take to snap you out of your funk?"

Flavius looked Davy right in the eyes. "You know darn well what it will take."

"Didn't I say we would head for home as soon as I saw the plains?" Davy reminded him. "All I want to do is ride on a ways and see me a buffalo. Once we do, I wish I may be shot if I don't turn around and light a rag for Tennessee."

"I'll believe it when I see it," Flavius said. As much as he liked and admired his companion, he was almighty tired of Davy's constant hankering to see what lay over the next rise or beyond the new horizon. He'd never met anyone so powerful curious about parts unknown.

Flavius had only himself to blame for being there, though. Weeks ago, when Davy first mentioned his notion of going on a gallivant, he could have declined. It was not as if Davy twisted his arm to make him tag along. No, he'd gone because he wanted to get away from his wife's constant nagging for a spell. Not to mention being spared the backbreaking chores she made him do from dusk till dawn six days a week.

"It shouldn't be long," Davy said. From the tales he'd heard, the prairie was crawling with buffalo. Lewis and Clark claimed to have seen herds so immense that it took hours for the thousands of great shaggy brutes to pass by. Now, *that* would be a sight! His hopes high, Davy surveyed the grassland from north to south.

Time passed, and Davy's hopes dwindled. Other than a few deer and a half-dozen buzzards that circled overhead for a while, there was no wildlife to speak of. It appeared that finding buffalo was going to be a lot harder than he had counted on. Just as he considered giving up, he spotted a high knoll to the northwest. From the top they would be able to see for miles. Reining toward it, he brought his mount to a gallop.

Flavius saw it too, and frowned. "Here we go again," he muttered under his breath.

They were sixty yards out when Davy detected movement at the knoll's base. Small animals, scores of them, were scurrying for cover. Some stood erect on two legs and whistled shrilly, a warning, he figured, for the whole colony.

The ground around the knoll was dotted with mounds of earth and more holes than a man could count. Davy slowed so his horse would not step in one of them. He could ill afford to have his horse break its leg.

Flavius's interest perked. He'd never seen any critters like these before. "What the blazes are they? Rats?"

"They look more like squirrels to me," Davy said.

But as they drew closer, it was apparent they were both off the mark. The animals were shorter than squirrels and thicker than rats. Their tails were similar to those of chipmunks, only longer. They would shake them when alarmed, then hold them stiff and straight when scampering into their burrows.

Flavius chuckled. "Look at 'em go! They sort of

remind me of my kin when the supper bell is rung. You never saw so much pushing and shoving."

Dismounting, Davy walked in among the dens. Every last animal had disappeared. A small head popped out of a hole a few yards away and just as promptly dropped from sight when the creature spied him. Its ears, Davy noticed, were like a squirrel's, only shorter, the fur fine and grayish.

"I bet they'd be downright tasty," Flavius commented. His stomach, as always, rumbled at the mention of food. "What say we kill five or ten for our supper?"

"You'd have to dig them out, and all we have to dig with are our hands," Davy noted. Sinking onto a knee, he peered into one of the burrows. It wound down into the bowels of the earth. "Would take us forever."

Flavius stepped to another hole and bent. "Maybe not," he said, imagining one of the critters roasted to a fine turn and garnished with wild onions. His mouth watered. "We could at least try." He stuck his nose close to the opening—and nearly jumped out of his skin.

A squat, broad face was inches from his own. Large unblinking eyes regarded him coldly. Flavius was so startled that he stiffened and made a stab for one of the two pistols that adorned the wide belt at his waist. "Land sakes alive!" he blurted.

Davy came over. The fattest toad he had ever beheld stared calmly up at them. It was so fat, it nearly plugged the hole. "There's your supper," he joked.

Flavius had momentarily lost his appetite. Toads and frogs and snakes and such were some of the few things he *wouldn't* eat. Truth was, creepy-crawly critters had scared the bejeebers out of him since he was knee-high to a nanny goat. "Not on your life!" he said. "That thing is ugly enough to gag a maggot."

Chuckling, Davy headed for the crest. He was halfway through the rodent village when suddenly a loud rattling noise broke out almost under his moccasins. The sorrel whinnied and shied, nearly yanking him off his feet before he could clamp hold of the bridle.

"Look out!" Flavius cried. Coiled at the mouth of a den was a big, dark rattlesnake, its scaly rattles quivering like a leaf in the wind. Flavius brought up his rifle.

"No!" Davy said, holding perfectly still. A shot would carry for miles, and there was no telling who might hear. Hostile tribes abounded on the plains.

The rattler might as well have been carved from stone. Other than its tail, it was motionless.

"You're taking an awful chance," Flavius whispered. He had the snake dead in his sights. All he had to do was squeeze the trigger.

"No," Davy repeated, praying the sorrel would not act up again.

The reptile abruptly shifted, and Davy saw a large bulge a third of the way down its body. It dawned on him that the snake must hunt the little squirrel-like creatures and have swallowed one not long ago. In which case it might be more inclined to crawl off to digest its meal than to attack.

The next moment the rattler proved Davy right by curling sinuously over its own body and slithering into a burrow. For a while they could hear the eerie crackle of its rattles, then there was welcome silence.

"We'd best keep our eyes skinned for more," Flavius said anxiously. The prospect of accidentally trodding on a snake covered him with goose bumps. He'd rather wrestle a painter bare-handed.

Davy nodded and walked higher. More careful from then on, he was almost to the end of the colony when swift motion to his right drew his attention to yet another animal the likes of which he had never seen before. This one resembled a weasel, but it had a tan coat and was black around the eyes. It also had a young rodent in its blood-flecked mouth. He lifted a hand to point it out to Flavius, but the thing disappeared down a hole with the quickness of thought.

Davy had to grin. Two new animals in two minutes. The day was looking up. Given that it was the shank of the afternoon, he hoped his luck would hold and they would spot some buffalo once they reached the top of the knoll.

As hills went, it was right puny. Only a hundred feet high, if that. Yet it towered over the surrounding flatland, so much so that when Davy gained the flat crown and paused, he was astounded by how far he could see. Even more riveting were the beasts grazing in a winding basin below and on the prairie beyond.

Davy had found his buffalo. He began to count them but stopped at two dozen. There had to be hundreds, strung out over half a mile or more, foraging contentedly on the sweet grass. Nothing he had ever seen had prepared him for the wonder of the experience. He'd been told they were huge, but he had not grasped exactly *how* huge.

They were enormous. Mighty, hairy brutes, as tall as a man at the shoulder, some probably weighing upward of two thousand pounds. Wicked curved horns framed massive, bony heads. Back in Tennessee, black bears had been the biggest animals around. Yet the buffalo dwarfed them.

Close to the knoll a bull was rolling on its back in a circular depression, caking himself with mud. Davy did not understand where the mud came from until he saw a different bull in another depression urinate on the dirt to moisten it, then roll around as the first one was doing.

For the life of him, Davy could not guess why they did it. Maybe it was for relief from the flies that swarmed over them like miniature dark clouds.

He saw many bulls, young and old. He saw cows. He saw calves. It boggled his brain to think that he was looking at enough meat on the hoof to feed the entire population of Tennessee for a whole winter.

Flavius was equally dazzled, and not a little frightened, besides. He could not help but wonder what would happen if the buffalo realized they were there. Would the bulls come after them? Maybe the herd would stampede. Fingering his rifle, he whispered, "Let's light a shuck while we can. I wouldn't want to rile those critters."

"Not so fast," Davy said, squatting. He was in no rush to spoil the moment. It made all the hardships they had endured along the way worthwhile.

As a boy, one of Davy's chief delights had been to roam the countryside just for the sake of seeing what he could see. He'd wandered near and far, covering more territory than most grown men. Always, the lure of the unknown had beckoned him on. It was safe to say that if he had not fallen in love and been forced to settle down, he might have wound up in California.

Not that Davy regretted either of his marriages. His first wife, Polly Finley, had been a precious darling who abided his quirks better than any man had any right to expect. It had devastated him when she died. For long months his soul had been in torment, a hurt soothed only when he met Elizabeth Patton, who was recovering from the loss of her first husband in the Creek War.

They were drawn together by their mutual grief, and their bond had grown from friendship to romance to wedlock in short order. Although each had children from their previous marriages, they were working heartily on a new crop.

Davy thought of his family now, and how much he missed them. Maybe Flavius was right, he mused. Maybe it was high time they bent their steps homeward. Elizabeth was a forgiving woman, but she might not take kindly to his being gone for so long when there were so many mouths to feed.

A grunt from close at hand brought an end to Davy's reverie. Glancing to his right, he was taken aback to see a bull buffalo not thirty feet away, lower down on the slope. It was regarding him intently, its head cocked, its nostrils widening.

"Don't move!" Davy cautioned his friend.

Flavius turned in the direction his partner was looking, but his horse blocked his view. Thinking that it must be another rattlesnake, he took a step past the dun, then felt his veins turn to ice. It was all he could do to keep from snapping off a shot. "Lordy!" he exhaled. "What if that monster gets his dander up? Let's light out while we can!"

"Hush!" Davy whispered as the bull took a few lumbering paces toward them, its broad back rippling with muscle, its horns glinting dully in the sunlight. He'd heard it said that full-grown bulls could bowl over a horse and rider with ease, and now that he had encountered one up close, he readily believed it.

Petrified, Flavius felt his palms dampen with sweat even as his mouth went dry. He licked his lips and wished the stupid animal would go elsewhere.

Instead, the bull stalked closer. It acted uncertain, tossing its head to better catch the breeze that fortunately was blowing from it to them and not the other way around. Snorting, it angled to the right until it stood between them and the herd proper.

Davy got the impression that this was an older animal, a sentry of sorts. Other old bulls ringed the perimeter of the herd, a first line of defense against marauding wolves and grizzlies, as well as roving human hunters.

For tense moments the outcome hung in the balance. The bull stopped sniffing and cropped some grass, leading Davy to conclude that the danger was past. The bull soon lost interest and moseyed off.

Just then, at the far end of the black mass, a commotion erupted. Yips and whoops rent the air. Figures on horseback appeared, streaking across the prairie toward the buffalo.

Appalled, Davy saw the herd break into motion, like a wave spawned by a stiff wind, sweeping eastward in a roiling mass of flying hooves and bobbing heads. Eastward, straight at the knoll.

"Oh, God!" Flavius wailed, forgetting himself.

"Ride like a bat out of hell!" Davy directed, suiting his actions to his words. As he vaulted onto the sorrel, the bull below them bellowed angrily, lowered its wide head, and raced toward them as if fired from a cannon. For something so huge, it moved incredibly fast.

Davy reined to the right to flee, then saw that his friend was in trouble. Flavius had hooked a foot in a stirrup and had a hand on his saddle, but the dun had spooked and was running in small circles, forcing poor Flavius to bounce alongside it like an oversize jackrabbit.

In another few seconds the bull would be on them. Davy cut to the left and hollered to draw the bull's attention away from his friend. It took the bait, slanting toward him while huffing and puffing like a runaway steam engine.

Davy flapped his legs and lashed the reins, goading the sorrel into breakneck flight. The bull gained rapidly, drawing closer and closer, so close that one of its horns swatted the sorrel's tail. It was a hand's width from the horse's hindquarters when the sorrel, in a burst of speed, pulled slightly ahead.

Bending low to the sorrel's neck, Davy glanced over his shoulder to check on Flavius. The last sight he had before his mount swept around the slope and down the far side was of Flavius keeling backward. He had to get back there and lend a hand before the stampeding herd reached the knoll.

But for the moment, it taxed Davy to merely stay alive. The bull was holding its own and showed no sign of giving up the chase anytime soon. Snorting noisily, the animal sent clods of dirt flying in its wake.

Davy tightened his grip on his rifle, which he had named Liz in honor of his second wife. In the distance he could hear thunder rolling across the grassland. Only it wasn't thunder. It was the drum of countless heavy hooves, growing louder second by second.

As much as Davy hated to stray far from Flavius,

his sole hope in eluding the bull lay in reaching the level land below, where the sorrel's stamina would stand him in good stead. Accordingly, he reined down the knoll, hell-bent for leather for the high grass.

Too late, Davy discovered that he had blundered. He was making for the rodent village, and there was no time to avoid it.

A single misstep might cost him not only the sorrel but also his life.

Heart in his mouth, Davy raced in among the holes and mounds. Almost immediately the sorrel's left foreleg came down dangerously near a burrow. Dirt cascaded from under the hoof, but the leg did not slide in.

Davy straightened so he would have a better chance of avoiding the dens. There were so many, though, that it was impossible for him to spot them all in advance. No sooner would he cut to the right or left to avoid one than another would materialize in his path. To make matters worse, something slid out from under the sorrel's front legs, inciting it to bound to one side as if it had springs on its legs. In landing, a rear hoof lodged in a hole. Davy braced for the crack of bone he was sure would ensue, but the horse pulled free with hardly any effort.

Two-thirds of the way across the maze, Davy heard a peculiar cry from the bull and the thud of its gigantic form crashing to the earth. He was elated to see that it had gone down, a hoof snagged by a burrow. The bull heaved to its feet, evidently unhurt, but by then Davy had a comfortable lead.

Reaching safe ground, Davy looped to the left. The bull had lost interest and was gouging the soil with its horns, almost as if it were taking out its frustration over losing him on the puny creatures that had caused it to trip.

Davy did not slacken his speed, even though he was in the clear. He had Flavius to think of. Rushing toward the crest, he could scarcely hear the pounding of the sorrel's hooves for the thunder of the onrushing herd. He estimated that he might have a minute to spare.

But he was wrong.

The sorrel was forty feet shy of the top when a brown wave rolled over it and spilled toward him. The roiling line extended hundreds of yards to the north and the south. Shoulder to shoulder, horn to horn, the living wall of steely sinew and bone hurtled forward.

Davy had no recourse but to rein completely around and ride for his life. He shuddered to think what might have happened to his friend. If Flavius had been unable to mount, the buffalo would have reduced him to so much pulp and busted bone fragments in the time it would take a person to spit.

That still might happen to Davy.

The herd was an immense juggernaut. Nothing could halt it. Nothing could withstand it. Even grizzlies would be swept under and trampled if they were overtaken.

As if to prove that point, from out of nowhere flashed three rabbits. Frantically racing for their lives, they bounded through the grass on either side of him, oblivious to his presence. A fox was next to appear, staring at the herd in abject fright before it, too, joined the exodus of the terror-stricken.

Davy veered to the left as he rode, trying to swing wide of the buffalo. A flock of grouse took wing, zipping off in a beeline to the west. So did several sparrows. He envied them their wings.

Sioux Slaughter

A shadowy shape lunged out of the grass, eliciting a nicker from the sorrel. Another shape joined it, then two more Davy had only a glimpse and decided they must have been wolves. The four of them ran into the open, enabling him to recognize them for what they were: coyotes. A male, a female, and a pair of cubs that would soon be on their own—if they lived long enough. Ordinarily they would have given Davy a wide berth. Under the circumstances, they paid him no heed. The herd was all that counted.

Davy twisted in the saddle. Dust choked the air above the stampeding bison, dust so thick it blotted out the sky, dust so heavy that it caked the humps and shoulders of the herd. For as far back as he could see, the plain was a swirling morass of hairy coats and horns.

Every second was a minute, every minute an hour. Davy tried not to think of what would occur should his horse go down. It would all be over in no time. His wanderlust could cost him his life, and might have already cost him the life of one of his very best friends.

Presently, the sorrel drew even with the east flank of the herd. A few more yards and Davy would be in the clear. He went those yards, and a dozen extra, leaving nothing to chance. Slowing and turning to the north, he watched closely as the front ranks drew abreast of him. It was the moment of truth. Would they break formation to come after him, or would they stay bunched together?

To say Davy was happy when the bison kept on going would be the understatement of the century. He slowed even more for the sorrel's benefit, putting a hand over his mouth as the spreading cloud of dust enveloped them. Fretting that he still might bump into a stray, he faced front just as a dark figure loomed out of the grass.

It was a horseman! Elated, assuming it to be Flavius, Davy uncovered his mouth and hollered his friend's name. That was when the dust briefly parted. Bearing down on him was not his friend, but a bronzed warrior armed with a bow, an arrow notched to the sinew string. As Davy gawked in surprise, the warrior brought the bow up and prepared to let his shaft fly.

Chapter Two

Flavius Harris did not have much patience with animals. It was a trait that he inherited from his pa, although he never went to the extremes that his father had.

Once, for instance, a horse had acted up when his pa was out plowing. It had refused to pull the plow and kicked his father in the leg so hard that the bone fractured. The doctor was called, and after he had applied a splint, Flavius's father had taken his rifle, gone out into the pasture, and shot that horse plumb dead.

Flavius never thought that had been right to do, even though the critter had acted up on him. He might take a switch to a dog that, say, chewed up one of his wife's quilts. Or he might whip a horse that tried to cave in his noggin. But he had never wanted to shoot a domesticated animal.

Until now.

With his foot caught in the stirrup and the dun

prancing around in circles as if it were putting on a show at the county fair, Flavius was mightily tempted to jam his rifle against its head and teach the dumb critter which one of them was the master.

Two things stopped him. One, there might not be another horse to be had for hundreds of miles around. Some tribes in the plains country had them, but just as many did not. And he had nothing to swap for one even if they located a tribe that did.

The second consideration was more crucial. Only an idiot would slay his sole means of salvation when a thundering herd of buffalo was bearing down on him.

So for the umpteenth time Flavius grabbed at the reins, which dangled under the dun, but missed. His trapped foot ached terribly from the strain and his free leg hurt from all the jumping he had been doing to keep up with the horse.

Meanwhile, the buffalo grew nearer and nearer.

Flavius deliberately did not look at them for fear he would be paralyzed with fright as he had been the time an uppity steer came at him in a pen back home. The quick thinking of his pa had saved him that day. Now there was no one to bail him out. Davy was gone, with a bull in hard pursuit. It was up to him to pull his fat out of the fire.

Mustering his strength, Flavius bent his leg and flung himself at the saddle. At last he was successful! He flopped across it, then shifted to sit up and stick his other foot in the other stirrup.

The horse picked that moment to flee. Nickering, it bolted to the south, Flavius clinging to its mane for dear life. "Whoa, boy!" he shouted, but the dun was not inclined to obey, not when the leading edge of the stampeding herd was less than sixty feet away and sweeping toward them like a living avalanche.

Flavius lunged at the reins. They swayed out of reach. That same second, the dun angled to go around the knoll. Flavius almost spilled off. Righting himself, he clamped his legs tight, tucked his rifle into the crook of his left elbow, and was content to let the horse do as it wanted.

But not for long. The dun was running parallel to the herd rather than away from it. That would have been fine if the herd were small and the dun could get past the outer fringe before the beasts plowed them under. The front ranks of this herd, though, extended for over a quarter of a mile in each direction. There was no way in hell the dun could outflank it.

His life hanging in the balance, Flavius made another stab at the reins. Somehow he caught hold. Smiling, he sought to turn the dun in the direction Davy had taken, but the stubborn horse refused to heed. He tugged harder. The dun finally turned, but by then it was too late. The herd was twenty feet behind them, gaining rapidly.

A lump formed in Flavius's throat. He was going to die! He knew it! It had been wrong of him to leave his wife and go traipsing all over creation, and now he was getting his just due.

Suddenly a gully appeared. It was narrow, shallow, and short.

Most men would have vaulted over and fled on. Flavius, acting on impulse, wrenched on the reins and jabbed his heels, compelling the dun to go down the side in a single bound. At the bottom Flavius leaped off, wrapped both arms around the animal's neck, his hands over its eyes, and, kicking at its forelegs, bore it to the ground so that it lay flat on its side with him on top.

23

Hardly a heartbeat later the herd reached the rim. Flavius glanced up. He nearly swooned at the sight of all those huge, hairy bodies, with their flying hooves, dilated nostrils, and wicked horns. Involuntarily, he tensed for the smash of heavy forms that were sure to rain down like hail.

None did. With nary a break in stride, the foremost buffalo leaped the gully and were gone. Those behind imitated the example of those in front. Buffalo after buffalo flew over Flavius's head, showering dirt and bits of grass upon him and filling the gully with so much dust that in short order Flavius could not see his hand in front of his face.

The ground shook and rumbled. It was like the time a few years back that an earthquake struck Tennessee, only worse.

A deafening din blistered his ears. Flavius licked his dry lips and tasted dirt. He hugged the dun, blinking against the dust, his heart hammering the walls of his chest as if striving to bust out.

The nightmare went on and on and on. Flavius lost all track of time. He had about convinced himself that he would live through the ordeal when a colossal crash to his right made him jump. A cow had fallen into the gully. Squinting, he could barely make it out as it struggled upright, then scrambled up the slope to merge with the cascading torrent of its brethren.

Afterward, Flavius was mortally afraid that another would smash down onto him and the dun. Every loud crunch, every spray of dirt, made him bite his lower lip to keep from crying out.

How long is eternity? For Flavius, that is exactly how long the stampede lasted. The constant drumming, the constant trembling of the earth, the constant cloud of dust left him dazed and exhausted, as if he had just run ten miles without a rest.

Abruptly, the thunder ended. It took Flavius a while to realize that the buffalo were gone. Sitting up stiffly, he listened in astonishment to the receding thud of hooves.

"I lived through it!" Flavius declared, flabbergasted, and regretted it when dust swirled into his mouth. Coughing and sputtering, he slowly stood. The dun sat up but did not try to stand.

Dreading that he might be mistaken, that more were yet to come, Flavius edged to the rim and took a peek. To the east roiled a gigantic brown cloud, dwindling into the distance. To the west the prairie was empty, a wide swath of grass laid bare, chewed up by thousands upon thousands of hooves.

Flavius was beside himself with joy. Bursting into laughter, he led the dun out and stood sucking fresh air into his lungs. His elation was short-lived, though.

"Davy?" Flavius said, pivoting three hundred and sixty degrees to scour the prairie. There was no trace of his friend. Cupping his hands to his mouth, he hollered, "Davy Crockett! Where are you?"

Silence answered him. Profoundly troubled, Flavius hastily brushed off the saddle and climbed up. If anything had happened—! He could not complete the thought. The consequences were too grave to contemplate.

Without Davy, Flavius knew he had scant hope of ever seeing his wife and kin again. He was not half the woodsman Davy was. His chances of reaching Tennessee alive by his lonesome were slim to none.

Anxiety eating at his insides, Flavius rode in a wide loop, seeking sign. He passed the spot where the odd little critters had lived. Their burrows were gone, reduced to loose piles of earth, every last hole obliterated. He speculated that the dens had caved in, smothering the poor things.

"Davy!" Flavius yelled. To the southeast, seemingly in reply, came a bawling cry. He trotted toward the source but saw no evidence of his companion or the sorrel. All he saw was a small mound of dirt. Dirt that unaccountably *moved*.

Flavius moved closer to find that it was actually a buffalo calf lying on its side. It probably tripped, he reasoned, and had been trodden by its fellows. He lifted the reins to resume his search, but hesitated when the calf raised its head and bawled at him.

The least Flavius could do was put it out of its misery. He hated to see anything suffer. He rode over, slid down, and hunkered. Not so much as a drop of blood smeared the earth. Not a solitary bone appeared to be broken. Flavius gingerly touched its flank. The calf did not recoil. He ran his hand over its back and sides, verifying that it was unhurt.

Perhaps it had been stunned, or merely fallen victim to exhaustion. The poor thing looked barely old enough to stand, let alone run.

"Well, you'll live," Flavius said. Relieved that he did not need to slit its throat, he rose.

The calf lurched to its feet, then mewed uncannily like a kitten.

Flavius chuckled. "Never knew buffalo could make that sound," he remarked. "But then, I never would have thought that painters can scream like women or that deer can cry like children if I hadn't of heard them with my own two ears."

He went to leave. The calf shuffled toward him and nudged his arm with its nose. Amused, he patted its head. "You're a sociable cuss, ain't you? But you'd better run along and catch up with your ma. Wouldn't want a mean old bear to find you alone or you'll wind up in its belly."

The calf stood there staring at him with wide dark eyes that were a lot like those of a puppy.

"Why are you looking at me like that?" Flavius said. "I can't hardly be bothered to tend to you when my best friend might be lying off on the prairie somewhere, busted to bits."

Once more Flavius made ready to mount. Once more the calf nuzzled him exactly as an affectionate dog would do. Annoyed, he pushed it, but the animal refused to budge. "Get along, now," he said gruffly. "There's nothing I can do for you."

The calf licked his hand, its tongue thick and rough and coated with slobber.

Flavius wiped his fingers on his leggings, forked leather, and swung the dun eastward. He had traveled a score of yards when the calf bawled one more time, stridently, like an infant afraid of losing a parent. "It won't work," he called back, and saw the animal doing its best to overtake him, its spindly legs pumping.

"Go away!" Flavius commanded, slowing. In short order the calf was ambling along next to his horse, its head tilted so it could observe him.

"I don't know what you aim to prove," Flavius said, common sense urging him to spur away and leave the young buffalo to fend for itself. "I'm not your nursemaid, if that's what you're thinking. I have more important things to do, you mangy idiot."

Flavius continued to ride, convinced the calf would tire after a while and he could get on with tracking down Davy unhindered. He tried to pay it no mind, but caught himself glancing down every few seconds. It was an adorable little cuss, he had to admit. Reminded him of a calf he had once taken a shine to on his uncle's farm. Hickory, he'd named it after it developed the habit of following him everywhere. He'd taught it to eat out of his hand and had brushed it every day.

"Foolishness," his pa had branded their antics. Later, when Hickory grew up and was sold to a butcher in Knoxville, Flavius had to agree.

"How about if I call you Little Hickory?" Flavius said, and then wanted to kick himself for what he had just done. Giving the buffalo a name was as stupid as allowing it to tag along, but he could not bring himself to gallop off and leave it. Not yet, anyway.

Flavius followed the herd eastward. It was long since gone, the rutted earth mute testimony to the destructive power that had been unleashed. To the northeast lay another calf. He bore toward it but changed his mind on seeing a pale spike of shattered bone jutting from the chest and a scarlet pool staining the earth.

A shadow flitted across him. Flavius bent his head, knowing what was up there. Five buzzards circled the dead calf, with more winging in from the west and the south, drawn to their grisly feast like metal to magnets.

More dots pinwheeled in the sky ahead. Flavius wondered if they marked the location of another dead buffalo, or Davy. He increased his speed, but not to the point where Little Hickory was unable to keep up.

The next body was larger than the other two had been. Either it was a full-grown buffalo or a horse. Flavius was glad to confirm the former, but he drew rein in consternation on seeing that from

28

this one protruded not splintered bone but three feathered shafts.

Indians! The word reverberated in Flavius's brain like the peal of a bell. He scanned the grassland for the owner of those arrows, but he was nowhere to be seen.

Not until that moment did Flavius vaguely recollect hearing whoops and shouts at about the same time the buffalo stampeded. At the time, he had been trying to get on the dun and had not paid much attention to anything else. Now he knew that a hunting party was in the area, and he fretted that Davy had fallen prey to them.

As different as Flavius and his friend were, they shared one trait. Unlike some whites who took perverse delight in exterminating every red man alive, neither Davy nor he had a hankering to tangle with hostile Indians unless the Indians left them no choice.

The Creek War was to blame. Flavius had joined up for the same reason as his friend: to teach the Creeks that they could not go around massacring white folks as they saw fit. He had been involved in a number of minor skirmishes, then had the misfortune to take part in the attack on the Creek town of Tallusahatchee.

Flavius had fought as well as any man in the company, but the savagery and slaughter had sickened him half to death. When his enlistment was up, he had gladly quit the army and gone back home to making his livelihood as a farmer.

Ever since, Flavius stayed shy of Indians who might be inclined to lift his hair.

From the stories told in taverns and saloons all across the frontier, Flavius gathered that the tribes west of the Mississippi were especially hostile to white men. They would as soon kill a frontiersman as look at him.

Little was known about them. Some were supposed to rely heavily on the buffalo for their subsistence. Certain tribes lived in established villages, while others roamed as they saw fit.

To the northwest lived the Flatheads, so named because the women allegedly tied boards to the foreheads of their infant offspring so that when the children were older, their heads were as flat as pancakes. Flavius was skeptical of the reports, but not of accounts about another tribe that dwelled far to the southwest. Apaches, they were called, bloodthirsty fiends who regarded anyone and everyone not of their people as bitter enemies. It was said that they derived intense pleasure from torturing captives for days on end.

Flavius had no illusions about how long he would hold up if he was caught by a tribe so disposed. He was brave enough when need be, but he did not possess the solid steel backbone Davy did. If tormented, he would weep and gnash his teeth and plead to be put out of his misery, something Davy would never, ever do.

Davy was canny in that regard. When faced with overwhelming odds or certain death, he would rather rely on his wits than his gun to get him out of trouble. But then, Davy was a born gabber. The man could talk rings around trees, a knack Flavius envied.

On more than one occasion Flavius had jested that Davy was so adept at spreading words around as if they were manure, he should go into politics.

"I wish I may be shot if I ever stoop so low," Davy was fond of responding.

Now, anxiously longing to rejoin the brawny Irishman, Flavius swung wide to the north, then back to the south, always on the lookout for tracks, repeating the pattern over and over for close to half an hour with no result. The calf stayed by him the whole time. When he stopped, it stopped. Whatever pace he set, it adopted.

"You must think I'm your mother," Flavius mentioned once.

An added worry was the growing lack of daylight. Soon the sun would set, leaving Flavius alone in the dark in the middle of the vast prairie. He'd rather swim across molten lava. Nighttime was when the predators were abroad: wolves, coyotes, painters, bears, and more.

"Oh, my," Flavius said softly. Not so much as a lick of cover was to be seen. He'd settle for a stand of trees or another gully. *Anything* that would offer some protection was fine by him.

To complicate matters, the calf showed signs of flagging. It dropped behind often and had to exert itself to catch up. Several times it bawled as if upset that they did not stop and rest. Flavius felt sorry for it, but he was determined to rove as wide an area as he could before the last light faded. Finding Davy was paramount.

Toward twilight a pack of skulking four-legged figures materialized to the north. Flavius mistook them for coyotes and did not give them another thought until one happened to sit on its haunches and howl.

They were wolves.

Flavius fingered his rifle. Normally wolves avoided humans, but he was in company with the calf, and buffalo calves were prime prey. The young and the old, the weak and the infirm, always were. It was Nature's way of ensuring that only the fittest survived.

The calf apparently detected their scent, because it bleated in fright and moved so close to the dun that the horse shied. Flavius had to keep a tight rein thereafter, never taking his eyes off the wolves for long. He grew perturbed when they showed no inclination to go hunt different prey. There were seven in all, a gray male in the lead.

"I should just ride off and let them have you," Flavius told the calf. "You don't mean diddly to me, critter." Yet he could not bring himself to do it. For better or worse, he would permit the calf to travel with him until he found Davy or they stumbled on some more buffalo.

The twilight began to deepen. Flavius had about resigned himself to making camp in the open, when to the south he discerned a break in the monotonous flat terrain. Whatever it was, it was bound to be better than no cover at all.

The calf balked at heading into the high grass. A swat on its rump with the reins sufficed to spur it to a basin approximately five acres across. Weeds and thickets choked the north bank.

Flavius sought a means down. A game trail served the purpose and he descended swiftly, aiming to get a fire started before full night sheathed them. He was only a few yards from the bottom when a piercing cry let him know that the calf had not followed. "What a yak!" he said, turning his mount. Just then the calf's bawling was drowned out by more bestial noises.

Specifically, the snarling of wolves.

Chapter Three

Davy Crockett could tell that the warrior was as startled by his sudden appearance as he was by the warrior's. About to loose a shaft, the man hesitated, scrutinizing Davy from head to toe. Davy seized the moment, flinging both arms over his head and saying, "Friend! I mean you no harm!"

It was a risky gambit. Some Indians, like some white men, were inclined to shoot strangers of another race at first sight.

The warrior was stout, young, and handsome. He wore his long black hair parted in the middle, braided on each side. A band of quilling ringed it at the top, while at the back were a pair of eagle feathers. Adorning his throat was a bear-claw necklace. He also sported shell earrings, which were unique for a warrior. His attire consisted of leggings, a breechclout, and moccasins.

That Davy did not try to shoot the warrior

seemed to make an impression. The man slowly lowered the bow partway, his eyebrows knitting in puzzlement.

Davy lowered his arms, careful not to point his rifle in the warrior's direction. "Friend!" he repeated in English, the Creek tongue, and the Ojibwa language. It was plain the man did not understand.

At a loss as to how to get his point across, Davy struck on the idea of placing Liz across his thighs, then clasping his hands together and accenting the gesture by smiling broadly and saying over and over, "Friends! Friends!"

Again the warrior merely sat there. After a bit he hesitantly set his bow across his lap, then did an odd thing. Holding his right hand in front of his neck with the palm out, he extended his index and second fingers and raised his hand until the tips of the two fingers were as high as his head. He looked at Davy expectantly.

Now, what was that all about? Davy wondered. It must be a hand sign of some kind, yet what it stood for eluded him. He shook his head to signify he failed to comprehend.

The warrior repeated the gesture. After waiting half a minute for a reply, he launched into a series of similar hand movements, his fingers moving so swiftly that Davy could not follow them. Again he looked at Davy as if anticipating a response.

"I'm sorry," Davy said. "I don't savvy. Where I come from the Indians don't do any talking with their hands. As for my kind, we love to hear the sound of our own voices too much for us to palaver any other way."

This time the warrior tossed his head. Unnotching the arrow, he slid it into a small quiver on his back. His horse, a young gelding built for speed and stamina, pranced in place as if eager to be off after more buffalo. The warrior kneed it forward, moving in a slow circle around the sorrel, inspecting everything but touching nothing. The rifle and pistol aroused the most interest. Davy's coonskin cap elicited a grin. On completing the circuit, the warrior motioned to the east, then beckoned for Davy to follow him.

Davy hesitated. To refuse might antagonize the man, but he had Flavius to think of. "I'd like to go with you, but I can't," he explained, even though the words were next to useless. "A friend of mine is back there somewhere." He pointed to the west.

The young warrior pointed eastward and once more beckoned.

"I'm sorry," Davy said, putting on a sad face to emphasize his meaning. "I have to find out if my partner is still alive." He started to rein the dun around, hoping the young man would not resort to weapons.

Suddenly two more warriors galloped out of the settling dust. Both were older than the first, and both held bows. At sight of Davy, they trained their arrows on him and the stockier of the pair, a surly specimen whose features were twisted in a perpetual scowl, snapped questions at the young warrior. Apparently the answers did not please him, for he glanced at the young warrior in blatant contempt.

Davy wished he had ridden off while he could. He had no doubt that if he so much as lifted a finger, those two arrows would be embedded in his chest quicker than he could blink. "I'm a friend!" he said when the surly warrior paused. "Can't you just let me go my own way in peace?"

35

Evidently not. The surly specimen bobbed his head and growled a few words.

Davy had the idea they wanted him to do something but no notion of what it might be. "I don't want any trouble," he stressed.

Without warning, the second newcomer nudged his mount closer, grabbed the end of Liz's barrel, and yanked. The rifle blasted, the ball striking the warrior low on the right side, flinging him from his horse and killing him.

It happened so fast, there was nothing Davy could do. He had lowered his right hand to surreptitiously cock the hammer when the newcomers appeared, and his finger was on the trigger when the gun was pulled. Since Liz had a hair trigger, all it took was the slightest pressure and she would discharge.

Aghast, Davy wheeled the sorrel. The fat was in the fire now. The Indians would never believe it had been an accident. He had to get out of there. But he had covered only ten feet when the surly one was on him.

The warrior did not fire. Instead, barreling in on his large roan, he deliberately rammed his mount broadside into Davy's. The collision jolted the sorrel sideways. It tripped, tottered, nearly went down, and it was all Davy could do to stay in the saddle. Somehow he accomplished it. He heard a war whoop and raised his head just as the surly warrior closed in, swinging a large knife. Its bone hilt connected with Davy's temple.

The world spun wildly. Davy struggled to stay conscious, flapping his legs to spur the sorrel out of there. His rifle began to slip from his fingers and he tightened his grip to keep from losing it. When a second blow caught him on the forehead, agony speared through him clear down to his toes.

A black cloud swallowed Davy like the big fish did Jonah. He was dimly aware of falling, of hitting the ground on his left side. After that he knew nothing for the longest while.

A swaying motion brought Davy around. His head throbbed so, he could hardly think. He was lying on his stomach. His hands and legs were bound.

Nausea eclipsed the pain. For a few moments he feared he would be sick, but the black cloud came to his rescue. Mercifully, it devoured him again.

How long Davy was out to the world, he did not know. His next sensation was of being jostled. There seemed to be voices murmuring all around him, but he chalked that up to his imagination. He passed out.

He awoke to the sound of a woman humming. For a while he lay still, listening, admiring the musical lilt to her voice. It must be Elizabeth, he thought. Funny that he had never heard her hum like that before.

Davy could not quite recollect where he was or what he had last been doing. He shifted, provoking a pang that seared him through and through and made him want to scream in anguish. In a rush of vivid memory his encounter with the three Indians came back to him. He remembered being hit. A groan nearly escaped his lips.

The humming stopped. Davy inadvertently flinched when a warm hand brushed his brow. The woman commented in a tongue he had never heard. He had a hunch that she knew he had come around, so he opened his eyes to behold one of the loveliest females in all creation.

She could not be more than twenty. Her hair was raven black, her face as smooth as marble.

She wore a dress of the finest buckskin decorated with beadwork on the front and on the sleeves. Kindly eyes mirroring keen intellect regarded him frankly, without the least hint of fear. Lips as red as cherries parted in a friendly smile as she withdrew her hand.

"Howdy, ma'am," Davy said. The effort sparked more pain. He reached up, his fingers finding a sizable gash on his temple and a welt on his brow.

The woman was on her knees beside him. Turning, she produced a moist cloth that she applied to his forehead, adding a gentle remark.

Davy sorely longed to know what she had said. Returning her smile, he stated, "I can't thank you enough for looking after me. You don't happen to speak my language, do you?"

It was a silly question. Resuming her humming, the woman turned to a small fire and leaned over a buffalo-paunch cooking pot.

They were in a lodge, but a lodge as different from those of the Creeks and Seminoles as night from day. Circular in shape, it was wider at the bottom than the top, and spacious enough for a family of four. Davy was lying next to the side. Running a hand over it confirmed that the dwelling had been fashioned from buffalo hides supported by long poles. At the top was an opening for smoke to escape.

Of equal interest were the furnishings. Around the lower third of the lodge hung a lining of some sort, gaily painted. Leather bags hung from the side or were piled where they were out of the way. A shield that bore the emblem of a buffalo had been propped near the entrance.

Firewood was stacked neatly. Near it was a wooden affair that might be a backrest. On the floor lay a bag that had spilled open, revealing a roll of sinew thread, bone awls, beads, and quills.

Davy heard a tiny gurgle. Around the woman crawled a small child, no more than a year and a half old. The boy was buck naked. He pushed a rounded stone, giggling when it rolled. "Hello there, sprout," Davy said.

The child halted. Wide, wondering eyes fixed on him. Cooing like a dove, the boy changed course, but he was scooped up by his mother before he could reach Davy.

Laughing lightly, the woman gave the child a playful shake and placed him flat on his back. He lay there as docile as a lamb while she dressed him, cackling when she tickled his ribs.

The scene reminded Davy of his own family. Elizabeth often frolicked with the children, tickling the younger ones until they begged for mercy. For a grown woman, she had a playful streak in her a mile wide. Several times she had enticed him into taking moonlit swims down at the river. The fact that he was always scared to death someone would stumble on them amused her to no end.

Davy idly slid a hand to his belt. It did not surprise him to discover that his knife and tomahawk were gone. So were his pistols, powder horn, and ammunition pouch. His cap was gone, too, and that peeved him. Unless he took the time to hunt down or trap a raccoon, he'd have to go without until he was home again.

Coonskin caps were popular with the backwoodsmen of states like Tennessee, Kentucky, and the Carolinas, but not, Davy had learned in his travels, with frontiersmen elsewhere. Which made no sense to him. In his opinion coonskin was superior to buckskin, wool, and ordinary leather when it came to shedding water and keeping his head warm on cold days. It also beat possum and skunk all hollow.

A pat on the foot brought Davy's reflection to an end. The boy, now dressed, amused himself by swatting Davy's moccasin as if it were a fly. "Better not inhale," Davy joked. "It's been a spell since I bathed last, and I'm liable to be getting a mite whiffy."

The woman was upending a water skin over a battered tin cup. She brought it to him, protesting when Davy propped himself on an elbow.

"I can manage," Davy assured her. Accepting the cup, he sipped, wondering where it had come from. The only way Indians obtained tin utensils was in trade with white men. Despite their unfamiliarity with English, her people must have been in contact with whites sometime in the past.

On the one hand, that was encouraging. If white trappers or traders came by on occasion, the tribe would be less likely to dispose of him.

On the other hand, the previous owners of the cup might have been slain just so the Indians could get their hands on the owner's possessions. In which case the tribe would not hesitate to kill him once it suited their purpose.

Davy worried about Flavius. Had his friend been caught in the stampede? Or had the Indians taken him captive, as well? When he finished the water, he handed the cup back. "I'm obliged," he said.

He decided to sit up. As the old saying went, he was not getting any younger. The sooner he established what the Indians had in mind, the better.

As if on cue, the front flap parted and in came the young warrior Davy had run into after the stampede. The man glanced first at the woman and the boy, the love he bore for them as plain as the nose on his face. The woman addressed him. His answer seemed to worry her.

Hanging his bow and quiver on the hide wall, the warrior approached the buffalo-hide bedding on which Davy had been placed. Again the man's fingers flew in a series of hand signs, which left Davy as baffled as before. When the warrior realized that Davy was at a loss, he sighed and hung his head, pondering.

Davy was not discouraged. He had always been a quick study once he put his mind to something, and it occurred to him that if the warrior was willing, he could learn enough of their peculiar finger talk to communicate. Accordingly, Davy tapped his chest, then held out his hands and wagged them up and down.

It took a bit for the warrior to divine his meaning. Actually, it was the woman who caught on first. Brightening, she spoke to her husband, who then pointed at Davy and held his right hand to the left of his face about level with his eyes. Index finger extended, he moved the hand from left to right, the finger passing across both eyes.

Wonderful, Davy mused. What did that mean? Did it pertain to him specifically? To white men in general? Or did it mean, maybe, "enemy"?

"Let's try this again," Davy said, indicating the little boy. In turn, he was shown the sign for the child, the woman, and the warrior, who warmed to the task once Davy caught on. Soon Davy was pointing at various objects in the lodge, and the warrior or the woman would reveal the sign for each.

That was all well and good. But knowing the sign for a shield or parfleche was one thing. Being

41

able to express questions and ideas was quite another.

The woman devoted part of her time to helping her husband and the rest to preparing a meal. Presently the heady aroma of boiling stew filled the lodge, reminding Davy of how famished he was. He was so hungry, his gut hurt. That alone hinted that he had been unconscious for quite a long time.

In addition to the stew, the woman served a boiled flour pudding made with dried fruit, and small cakes of a type unknown to Davy. He wolfed his portions with relish. Water sufficed to wash it down.

Coffee would have been preferable, but Davy saw no evidence of any in the lodge. He had not noticed previously, but some of the hides that composed the lodge wall were in need of repair. Several of the parfleches had also seen better days. A blanket on which the child played was faded and frayed.

The couple were just starting out in their married life. Many of the items scattered about the lodge must be from relatives. Hand-me-downs, whites would call them.

By anyone's standards, the pair were hardly well-to-do. Yet they were willing to share what little they had with a perfect stranger. Their generosity and kindness deeply impressed Davy.

It made him think of some of the contrary settlers Flavius and he had met during their journey, people who refused to allow them so much as a sip from a well or a tiny piece of bread.

The young couple were prime examples of the truth that it wasn't the color of a person's skin that determined whether they were good or bad. Every basket, as the saying went, had a few rotten apples.

Through a gap at the entrance Davy saw that it would soon be dark. He also glimpsed other lodges and a wide stream or river. As near as he could tell, all the dwellings faced east. There must be significance to that, but he did not know what it might be.

Suddenly the beat of a drum sounded. A man shouted at some length, apparently making an announcement. Seconds later the drum beat came again, only farther away. The same announcement was repeated.

The warrior and his wife looked at each other. Their expressions revealed that they were nervous, and in silence they listened as the crier went about the whole village.

Davy was mystified. What did they have to be nervous about? He was the captive, the one who might not live to see the light of a new day. He lay back down to rest and think, but no sooner did he do so than a different voice called out, just past the entrance. The woman instantly picked up her child and scooted to the rear. The warrior took a seat on the other side of the fire, facing the flap, then responded.

Into the lodge came three warriors. One was the surly polecat Davy owed for the gash and the welt. The other two were new to him. One was broad-shouldered and wore an elaborate headdress; the other was short and gray-haired. The latter gave him a kindly smile, but the surly warrior rubbed the hilt of the knife he had struck Davy with.

A short talk ensued. The young warrior acted displeased by what was said and twice glanced unhappily at Davy. Not once was the woman consulted.

None of the words made a lick of sense to Davy, except one. Toward the end, the short man used the word *Nadowessioux*. It was French, used in connection with a tribe more commonly known as the Sioux or Dakotas. Little was known about them, other than that they were heavily dependent on the buffalo for their livelihood and they were reputed to be highly warlike.

Shortly, the three men departed. The husband and wife huddled together, casting frequent glances at their guest.

Davy gathered that he had been the subject of the meeting, and that something was about to happen that would decide his fate. He was confronted with the choice of letting circumstances take their course, or of somehow giving his captors the slip.

An added problem was that Davy would not think of laying a finger on the couple who had befriended him, even though it would be relatively easy to knock both of them out and light a shuck before the rest of the tribe realized what had happened.

The warrior moved to a parfleche and took out a folded set of superb buckskins. They were probably the best clothes he owned. He stripped, then donned them, and traded in his old moccasins for a pair that seemed to have been recently made.

Davy gauged the distance to the entrance. He could be out it in three bounds. But the sound of muffled voices outside convinced him that many people were still abroad. He would be lucky if he got ten feet before they brought him down.

The issue was made moot when the young warrior stood, strode to the entrance, and motioned.

"Any chance of more pudding first?" Davy quipped. "I hate to be put to death on an empty

44

stomach." As he rose, the woman came over bearing his coonskin cap, freshly cleaned. Delighted, he squeezed her hand to show his thanks since he did not yet know the proper sign for that. He made a mental note to learn.

The scent of wood smoke hung heavy over the village. Although the sun was gone and by rights most of the inhabitants should be in their lodges relaxing after their evening meal, the majority were outdoors, gathered close to their dwellings, as if awaiting a signal.

All eyes swiveled toward Davy as the young warrior led him toward a lodge much larger than the rest. Only then did it occur to Davy that the Sioux had been waiting for *him*. He was the sole focus of attention from the moment he appeared until he reached the entrance to the big lodge.

Feigning a casual air, Davy beamed and nodded at everyone he passed. It was a calculated ruse on his part. Just in case the people had a say in what their leaders did with him, he wanted them to think that he was the friendliest white man they'd ever run across.

At the buffalo-hide flap, the young warrior hesitated and seemed loath to enter.

Davy took that as a sign that whatever was in store for them in there would not be to his liking. Davy glanced at a little girl who gaped at him as if he had two heads; then he spotted a horse fifteen feet away at the side of the large lodge. It was a magnificent stallion and it wore a rope bridle. Best of all, no other horses were anywhere near it. Someone had been mighty careless.

Davy had to time it just right. Some of the Indians were converging on the lodge; he dared not let them get too close. The young warrior tapped his arm, stooped, and went in. Davy bent to do the same. But instead he hurtled around the lodge to the stallion and executed a flying jump onto its back.

Excited yells broke out. Davy ignored them. Smacking his legs against the stallion's sides, he made his bid for freedom.

Chapter Four

The seven wolves had backed the buffalo calf up to the brink of the basin rim. Ringing their prey, the pack snarled hungrily as their big gray leader stalked toward the calf.

It was on this scene that Flavius Harris burst after galloping up the slope. His arrival scattered the wolves right and left, except for the leader, which skipped aside and nipped at the dun's hind legs. Twisting, Flavius tried to fix a bead, but the wolf would not stand still long enough. It danced to the right, reversed itself, and sprang at Little Hickory like a bolt of lupine lightning.

The calf tried to bolt out of the way, but it was abysmally slow. It bawled in panic as the wolf slammed into its shoulder, driving it farther back. For a few seconds it teetered. Then, spindly legs flailing awkwardly, it regained its balance.

The same could not be said for its attacker. As the wolf cut to the left to set itself for another at-

tempt, the earth under its paws gave out. Scrab-
bling furiously for support that was not there, the
predator tumbled down the bank into a heavy
thicket.

Flavius moved as near to the edge as he could
and rose in the saddle to peer into the brush. Like
a ghostly specter, the big wolf had vanished.
Swinging the dun, Flavius sought the others. They
were off in the tall grass somewhere. The calf was
trembling but otherwise appeared to be unhurt.

"Serves you right for falling behind," Flavius
chided. "Now, come along." Going to the game
trail, he paused to verify that the calf was following this time, then rode back down into the basin.
He did not like that the vegetation hemmed them
in on both sides. So little light was left that the
wolf could be on them before he got off a shot.

Thankfully, the big gray did not appear. Flavius
went a dozen yards from the growth and halted.
After ground-hitching the dun, he hurried to a
thicket to collect an armful of broken limbs and
as much dry grass as he could carry. Three trips
were enough to provide a sizable pile that he figured would last him for hours.

The calf cropped grass. Flavius was glad it was
old enough to do so, or the poor thing would
starve for want of its mother's milk.

From his possibles bag Flavius took his steel
and flint, then his tinderbox. It was half filled
with his favorite type of punk, namely dry, de-
cayed maple.

He applied a small amount to the kindling, then
struck the flint a slicing blow with the steel, pro-
ducing a shower of sparks. Not being as adept as
Davy, it always took him about seven to ten tries
before he got the punk going. Bending, he blew
lightly on the tiny flames, fanning them, adding

kindling as needed until he had a warm, cozy fire crackling brightly.

As the flames rose, Flavius kept an eye on the calf, afraid it would bolt into the gathering gloom. He might not be able to find it again. But the wolves certainly would.

Much to his surprise, the calf displayed no fright. It stared at the fire with those wide, child-like eyes for the longest while, as if mesmerized. Finally it resumed cropping grass, its small tail twitching.

Flavius had to settle for jerky. He munched morosely while stripping the dun and arranging the blanket and saddle into a fairly comfortable bed.

Truth to tell, Flavius was sick to death of jerky. Davy and he had packed plenty for their gallivant, most supplied by Davy's wife. She had a way of flavoring the dried meat so that it tasted like honey, and at first Flavius could not get enough of the stuff. Davy had to remind him again and again that it was supposed to last the entire trip, or he would have devoured it all within the first few days.

Since Davy intended to live off the land, they had packed light. No coffee. No flour. No sugar. This last item Flavius missed the most. He had a passion for it that defied reason.

What he wouldn't give right then for a piping hot cup of coffee with five or six spoonfuls of sugar added! The thought made his mouth water.

A muted crack brought Flavius back to reality. Placing a hand on one of his pistols, he scanned the north side of the basin. By now it was so dark, the thickets were an inky mass silhouetted against the lighter backdrop of the grass and the sky.

Flavius had counted on the fire driving the pack away. It always worked back home in Tennessee.

But either these wolves were famished enough not to give up, or they were a different breed than the wolves he was accustomed to.

Placing his rifle beside him and loosening both pistols so he could draw them swiftly, Flavius reclined on the saddle. He wasn't overly worried. The wolves could prowl the thickets all they wanted, so long as they kept their distance.

He doubted they would be rash enough to venture into the open. If they did, the dun would alert him. So long as he maintained the fire and had ample light to shoot by, the horse and calf and he should be safe.

Until that moment Flavius had not realized how tired he was. His eyelids grew leaden, his limbs sluggish. Yawning, he fought off sleep for another fifteen minutes. Just as he dozed off, something brushed against his leg.

Snapping up, Flavius fumbled for a pistol, then stopped and broke out in a wide grin. Little Hickory had ambled over and plopped down next to him. Chortling, Flavius stroked its neck and scratched behind its ears.

"You're worse than a damned dog," Flavius complained, although inwardly he was tickled pink. The buffalo licked his hand again.

"You're wasting your time," Flavius said. "I refuse to get attached to you. You're only going to die sooner or later, just like the original Hickory."

Lying back, Flavius covered his eyes with a forearm and listened to the snap and crackle of the burning branches.

He wasn't much for deep thinking, but it had always bothered him how the world was set up. Seemed to him that there was entirely too much suffering.

Why did the Lord allow sickness and accidents

and the like? What purpose did it serve for folks who had never harmed a living soul to be afflicted by disease and have to endure torment? Why were wicked people allowed to ride roughshod over decent ones?

It was a mystery Flavius could never fathom, even though he read Scripture regularly. Or, rather, Matilda read it to him, since she was a stickler for reading at least one passage from the Bible every day.

Some parts were easy for Flavius to understand. "Thou shalt not steal" was as plain as could be. But then there was that other Commandment, "Thou shalt not kill." All well and good, but what was a man to do when a war party of hostiles besieged his cabin and threatened to wipe out his entire family? And if it was not right to kill, why, then, in Ecclesiastes, did it state that there was "a time to kill, and a time to heal"?

Life was the darnedest puzzle ever, and Flavius was at a total loss as to how to solve it.

Part of the fault lay in him. Never one to deceive himself or others, Flavius was all too aware that he was not exactly the smartest gent alive. He often wished he were, because then all the answers would come to him.

Or would they?

Davy had five times the brains he did, yet even Davy admitted to sometimes being as stumped as he was.

Maybe people weren't supposed to understand life. Maybe it was *meant* to be a puzzle. Maybe—

A low growl fell on Flavius's ears. With a start, he realized that he had drifted off.

The growl was repeated. Opening his eyes, Flavius was horrified to see that the fire had almost burned out. He had slept for hours. A few flickering fingers of flame were all that were left. The wolves would close in soon unless he built the fire up again.

Flavius froze. The wolves had already closed in. Five of them formed a semicircle fifteen feet away, their hunched forms a prelude to a concerted rush. Prominent among them was the big gray male, its eyes glowing red like burning coals.

Little Hickory slumbered blissfully on, exhaustion dulling its senses.

Why hadn't the dun whinnied? Flavius wondered, rotating his head just enough to learn that the dun was gone. The missing wolves must be after it. Maybe, Flavius mused, it had tried to warn him but he had not heard.

The big male wolf slunk forward, its glowing eyes lending it the aspect of demon spawn. Its teeth gleamed as it vented a bloodthirsty snarl.

Flavius rose higher and the wolf stopped. He still had a chance to get out of there. It was the calf the pack wanted. They would probably not interfere if he were to slowly stand and back off.

That very moment Little Hickory rolled over, facing him. The calf's eyelids fluttered. Its mouth made a smacking noise, as it would if it were sucking on one of its mother's teats.

Flavius could not move. The calf was so like a sleeping infant that he would never be able to live with himself if he deserted it. His presence was all that had spared it so far from the searing claws and teeth of the ravenous pack. Some folks might call him stupid for sticking, but they weren't the one standing there with five slavering predators inching steadily closer.

"You picked the wrong meal," Flavius declared, drawing both flintlocks and cocking them.

The sound of his voice caused two of the wolves

to whirl and bolt. The big male did the opposite. Uncoiling, it sprang at Little Hickory just as the calf woke up and rolled over.

The wolf was in midair when Flavius stroked both triggers. Twin balls cored its body, flinging it to the ground as if it had been slammed into by an invisible fist. The other two wolves, in the act of charging, broke to the right and the left and whisked into the night.

They were not the only ones. Little Hickory, terrified by the blasts and the smoke, scrambled erect and sped off across the basin, bawling his lungs out.

"No!" Flavius hollered, to no avail. The calf was panic-stricken. Tucking the pistols under his belt, he grabbed his long rifle and jogged after it. He disliked leaving his saddle and blanket behind, but the calf's welfare came first. Huffing and puffing, he covered a hundred yards without spying hide nor hair of Little Hickory.

Winded, Flavius stopped to catch his breath. "Where the dickens are you?" he groused. The calf had to be close by. Scant cover existed on the south side of the basin, but it was so dark that Flavius could not distinguish objects more than a half-dozen yards off.

Flavius walked on, turning right and left, anxious to get back to camp and rekindle the fire. He needed light to reload the flintlocks. Some frontiersmen, like Davy, could load their guns in the dark, but that was a feat Flavius never had gotten the hang of.

A man had to add just the right amount of black powder for a pistol or rifle to discharge properly. Too little, and the ball might as well be fired from a slingshot. Too much, and the barrel could burst.

In the dark, Flavius was never sure of doing it properly.

A hint of movement off to the right brought Flavius up short. Was it the calf or the dun? Or perhaps a wolf? Cocking the rifle, he crouched low, as Davy had taught him. At night a man could see better lower to the ground than when standing.

He was rewarded by the sight of a four-legged form pacing back and forth at the very limits of his vision. From its size and shape, it had to be a wolf.

"Persistent cusses," Flavius muttered.

As tempting as it was to shoot, Flavius saved his ball in case he needed it more later on.

The wolf melted into the gloom, so Flavius rose and continued to the south slope, his legs swishing the high grass with every step. Little Hickory did not appear. Dejected, Flavius roved the basin perimeter until he reached the heavy growth on the north side. No telltale growls greeted him. The pack had apparently gone, too.

That was not a good sign.

Shaking his head to dispel horrid images of the helpless calf being ripped to shreds by slavering fangs, Flavius made for the wisps of smoke that rose from the campfire. He was almost there when it hit him that something else was now missing. His bedding was intact. His possibles bag had not been touched. What else could it be?

A chill rippled down his spine as he realized it was the big gray wolf.

"Impossible!" Flavius blurted, darting to the spot where the wolf had fallen. Dark stains marked the soil. Hunkering, running his fingers over the soil, he detected scrape marks where the predator had dragged itself off into the brush.

Wild animals were strange in that regard. They never wanted anyone or anything to see them die. They would rather expire by their lonesome than do it even in the company of their own kind. Mortally stricken, they found a quiet spot, curled up, and surrendered the ghost. If animals had one.

Certain he had seen the last of the big wolf, Flavius got the fire going. His next order of business was reloading. When that was done, he stretched out on his back and treated himself to another small chunk of jerked venison.

He was in a fix now, for certain. Davy was gone, possibly dead. The dun had run off. He was lost in unknown country with little food and only the clothes on his back and a few dozen lead balls to see him through until he reached a settlement. Were he a gambling man, he would not wager a red cent on his prospects.

Flavius tried to console himself by noting that it did no good to cry over spilt milk. He had to make the best of the situation. In the morning he would head east until he struck the wide river that Davy and he had crossed several days ago. He believed it was the Mississippi, but Davy was inclined to think it was the Missouri. Whichever, once across, Flavius would head southeast until he came on some white folks.

Easy as pie.

Pulling his blanket up to his chin, Flavius grasped a pistol in each hand and tried to sleep. This time it was not so simple. His overwrought nerves would not permit him the luxury.

The beastly chorus in full throat outside of the basin did not help much, either. Wolves were constantly wailing their plaintive cries. Coyotes yipped without cease. As if that were not enough, the guttural grunts of prowling grizzlies, the scream of panthers, and the bleat of victims punctuated the din from time to time.

Flavius tried to get to sleep by counting the stars, but he soon developed a kink in his neck. He counted sheep next, a ruse that had worked when he was small, so maybe it would again. He was at fifty-eight when slumber claimed him.

The warm sunlight on his face woke Flavius out of a sound sleep. Feeling refreshed but lethargic, he stretched and rolled onto his back without opening his eyes. A few more minutes of rest would do him good.

It had been ages since Flavius was last able to sleep past sunrise. Matilda was a stickler for being up and about at the crack of dawn, always scolding him for being a lazy layabout when he tried to catch a few extra winks. Davy had turned out to be just as fanatical about rising early, a habit he had acquired as a child.

Let them get up with the crows if they wanted! For once Flavius could do as he pleased, and it pleased him to sleep until he was tired of sleeping!

Flavius smiled, then went rigid as something wet and raspy stroked the left side of his face. Shocked, he looked up just as a large pink tongue descended, slobbering across his nose and lips.

"Consarn it!" Flavius fumed, getting some of the slobber into his mouth in the process. Spitting and sputtering, he sat up as he was licked a third time, on the ear.

"Enough, for land sakes! You're drowning me!" Flavius said, pushing off the ground. Wiping his sleeve across his face, he held out an arm to prevent Little Hickory from doing it again. The calf was wagging its tail just like a dog, and looked as happy to see him as he was to see it.

"Where have you been?" Flavius asked, checking the calf for wounds. "I was worried sick that those mangy wolves got you."

The calf playfully nuzzled him. Flavius laughed and gave it a smack on the rump. Little Hickory bounded in a circle, bucking like a mustang, then prepared to butt him.

"Hold on, junior!" Flavius cautioned. "One of us might get hurt, and it could be me." The calf's horns had started to grow but were as yet mere knobs. Another six months and it would be a different story.

Flavius ran a hand through his hair, plastering it to his head. He double-checked that his guns were loaded, then scratched his chin, debating whether to lug the saddle and blanket along or to cache them until he could come back.

A whinny to the west spared him from having to decide. The dun had not strayed far, after all. After stomping its front hoof a few times, the horse trotted into the basin and slowly approached.

Flavius stood stock-still. Experience had taught him that if he ran toward the contrary animal, it would run off. He had to make the horse think that he could not care less if it came close, and then it would. Sure enough, without his lifting a finger or raising his voice the dun pranced up to him and permitted him to grip the bridle.

"From here on out I hobble you," Flavius vowed. Normally he would have scolded the horse for running off, but having both the calf and the dun return safe and sound had put him in mighty fine spirits.

"It must be my lucky day." It amused Flavius that he was talking to the animals as he would to Davy. If his mother-in-law could see him now, she'd claim he was touched in the head.

David Thompson

Saddling up, Flavius mounted and headed for the game trail that would take them to the top. Things were going so well that he entertained high hopes of finding the buffalo herd before long. As for Davy, Flavius could not shake a nagging fear that his friend had met a violent end.

It would not be the first time Flavius had lost someone he cared about.

Life on the frontier was nothing if not harsh, and those who chose to live in the deep woods learned early on that Nature was a temperamental mistress. Violence was a daily part of their existence, wild animals, hostile Indians, and the elements themselves usually to blame.

Death was a common occurrence, and if a person was too cocky for their own good, or too careless at the wrong moment, or just plain stupid, they died that much sooner. With that thought in mind, Flavius came to the gap in the brush that marked the game trail and swung into it. A gasp ripped from him.

Coming down the slope toward him was a grizzly.

Chapter Five

Davy Crockett, smirking in triumph, lashed the reins of the stallion and hunched forward in anticipation of making a rush for the prairie. The stallion, though, just stood there as if it were carved from stone.

Boisterous mirth cascaded through the village. All the Dakotas were fit to bust a gut. Not one raised a weapon against him or tried to grab the horse before it ran off.

With a sinking feeling in his stomach, Davy glanced down. The stallion's forelegs were hobbled. He could smack it until Judgment Day and they would not go anywhere. His ruddy cheeks growing redder, Davy sheepishly slid down and rejoined the young warrior, who was the only person in sight not laughing. "Sorry," Davy said. "It seemed like a right smart notion at the time."

A small boy nearby mimicked his antics by dashing to a stick, wedging it between his legs, and pretending to lash it as Davy had the stallion. A renewed torrent of glee rippled through the encampment.

"It's nice that your people appreciate a good laugh," Davy told the young warrior.

It would have been nice to be able to speak his newfound friend's name, and earlier he had tried to do just that, without much success. It was a real tongue-twister.

There was another problem: the language barrier. As fast as Davy was picking up the sign language used by the tribe, he still could not express or grasp complicated concepts. The young warrior's name had proven difficult because one of the words had been particularly hard for the man to convey.

As near as Davy was able to comprehend, the warrior was known as White-Hollow-Horn. Or it might be White-Empty-Horn. Or even White-Hole-Horn, although Davy thought the last extremely unlikely.

Now, as White-Hollow-Horn parted the flap and went in, Davy took a deep breath to steel his nerves. He had to keep his wits about him at every moment from now on. Whatever occurred next would determine whether he lived or died.

The lodge was twice the size of White-Hollow-Horn's. Fourteen warriors were present, dressed in what had to be their very finest garb. At their head sat a powerfully built warrior Davy had not seen before, an imposing individual who sat straight and proud.

That would be the high chief, Davy reckoned, the man who had the most say, the man whose advice the rest of the tribe was apt to follow, and therefore the man Davy most had to impress.

Also present were the three warriors who had

paid White-Hollow-Horn a visit.

Surly Face, as Davy nicknamed him, was one of those seated nearest the entrance. Since it was common among the Creeks and Seminoles for the warriors of highest standing to sit nearest their leader, Davy wondered if maybe the Sioux did the same. In that case, Surly Face was low in rank, which was a plus for Davy in that Surly Face's opinion would not count for all that much.

The warrior with the wide shoulders sat about halfway up the row on the left, while the gray-haired warrior with the kindly eyes sat at the chief's right side.

White-Hollow-Horn led Davy between the two rows and halted in front of the high chief. Davy held his chin high and would not allow his face to betray a lick of anxiety. As he had learned during the Creek War, Indians regarded courage as a supreme virture. They respected bravery even in their enemies.

The high chief addressed White-Hollow-Horn, whose answer, complete with pantomime, demonstrated that the chief had asked about the commotion outside. When White-Hollow-Horn got to the part where Davy had whipped the stallion to get it going, fully half of the assembled leaders laughed heartily. One of those was the gray-haired warrior.

Davy smiled at the man, then shrugged his shoulders and rolled his eyes skyward. That made the old warrior laugh harder. Davy suspected that he had made another friend, and he could only hope the older man's influence would help him out when it came time for the council to render a decision as to his fate.

At a gesture from the grand chief, White-Hollow-Horn sank onto his knees. Davy, without being told, did the same, and added a courteous bow to the high chief.

The council began. Initially, White-Hollow-Horn and Surly Face did most of the talking. Davy gathered that they were telling about his capture. At one point a heated exchange erupted between the pair, stopped only when the high chief interceded.

Then White-Hollow-Horn had another warrior extend an arm. Yanking on it, he voiced a loud cry and pretended to fall. Whatever he added did not please Surly Face, who curtly interrupted and went through the motions of deliberately firing a rifle.

Davy did not need an interpreter to understand. They were arguing over whether the shooting of their companion had been an accident or intentional. No one had indicated he could speak, but he felt it best to get across his side of the dispute. Pointing at White-Hollow-Horn, he made the sign for "yes." Shifting, he stabbed a finger at Surly Face and signed an emphatic "no."

Murmuring broke out. The high chief asked Davy a question in sign language. Most of the gestures were ones Davy had yet to learn, but he got the gist. The chief had asked him if he was fluent in sign. "No," he answered, and qualified it by making the hand symbols for "little sign."

It sufficed. The high chief addressed White-Hollow-Horn. Next the gray-haired man spoke. Others had their turn. A decision of some kind was being made, and Davy was on pins and needles waiting for them to make their verdict clear. If they chose to slay him, he was going to make another break for it, on foot this time. He would rather go down fighting than be hog-tied and led out like a lamb to the slaughter.

The Crockett clan were not the kind to die meekly. Ingrained in their Irish heritage was a fighting spirit that had seen them through countless conflicts in their native Ireland and in the New World as well. Davy's grandpa had borne a scar on his left side inflicted by an enemy's sword in the Old Country. Davy's pa had been a frontier ranger during the American Revolution.

No, Davy would not be slain without a fight. Even though the odds were hopeless, he would show the Sioux that Crocketts were warriors in their own right.

The council went on and on. Every man was given a chance to speak his piece. When it was Surly Face's turn, he harangued them at length, casting many spiteful glances at Davy. In conclusion, he indicated Davy and raised his right hand in front of his right shoulder with the hand nearly closed, then chopped his hand down and to the left.

It was a sign Davy had not been taught, but its meaning was not hard to guess. Surly Face had recommended that he be rubbed out.

Two last warriors had their say, then, when they were done, everyone turned their attention to the high chief, whose forehead was furrowed in thought.

Davy could feel sweat on his palms. His welfare rested in the hands of a man who had sufficient reason to have him slain. Killing a warrior was a severe offense. Many Sioux besides Surly Face were bound to resent it.

Everything depended on the high chief's sense of justice and fairness.

The silence was thick enough to slice with a tomahawk. Davy had to exert all his willpower to keep from fidgeting. When the leader gazed at him, he met the gaze frankly and fearlessly. An eternity passed while the chief appeared to take his measure.

Everyone listened when the leader rendered his decision. Some of the warriors, such as the gray-haired man and White-Hollow-Horn, smiled. Surly Face and a few others looked fit to choke. All of which seemed to be a good sign.

White-Hollow-Horn rose and beckoned Davy. Once outside, the young warrior visibly relaxed. Dozens of Sioux were clustered near the main lodge, evidently awaiting word. White-Hollow-Horn responded to something a fellow warrior said, and his answer was rapidly relayed from person to person.

Davy could barely contain himself. He had to find out what the chief had decided. The moment they were back in White-Hollow-Horn's lodge, he nudged the young warrior and arched his eyebrows.

It was Davy's fervent hope that he would be released unharmed. But that was not to be. The leader, whose name translated as Black Buffalo, had instructed White-Hollow-Horn to teach Davy enough sign language for Davy to speak on his own behalf at the next council. There was only one hitch: The next council would be held in three days.

Davy supposed he should be grateful for the temporary reprieve, but all he felt was keen disappointment. Glumly taking a seat on his bedding, he rested his chin in his hands and debated whether to wait out the three days or try to escape.

The young couple became embroiled in an earnest discussion, the woman upset about something or other.

Davy was sorry to be such a burden on them.

After all they had done on his behalf, the last thing he wanted was to cause them any grief. That alone was enough of a reason for him to leave as soon as he could.

Another had to do with Surly Face, who was bound to spend the next three days stirring up sentiment against him. Popular opinion being as fickle it was, Surly Face might succeed in turning everyone against him. Should that happen, the high chief would have no choice but to have him put to death.

It was a no-win proposition. Even if he got away, the Sioux were bound to come after him. Unless he was uncommonly lucky, he'd wind up their prisoner again.

The more Davy pondered, the more hopeless it seemed. But he had to do it, so there was no use moaning and groaning. If by some miracle he eluded them, he would spend however long it took to track down Flavius and grant his friend's long-deferred wish to head for home.

Outside, someone called out. White-Hollow-Horn rose and bid them enter. Davy stiffened when Surly Face and three other warriors came in, Surly Face wearing a wicked sneer and holding an old pair of rusted leg irons. Where in the world the Sioux had obtained them, Davy did not know.

Another brief argument took place, White-Hollow-Horn objecting to what Surly Face had in mind. Evidently the high chief had given his consent, because the young warrior reluctantly stepped aside.

Davy rose. "If you think you're slapping those shackles on me," he snapped, "then think again." Once in irons, he would be helpless. Escape would be impossible.

Grinning sadistically, Surly Face shook the

chains so they rattled noisily. The three men with him fanned out, one blocking the entrance. None of them resorted to weapons. But then, they had no need. All three were muscular and strong.

White-Hollow-Horn protested once more, but Surly Face brushed him away in blatant contempt. Turning to Davy, the young warrior signed, in effect, "You must let them do as they want or they will harm you."

Crouching, Davy said, "Let them try!" He bunched his fists, eager to plant one on the tip of Surly Face's nose. The four warriors inched forward, Surly Face swinging one of the shackles in a small circle to taunt him.

"Come on, you bastard!" Davy fumed.

Surly Face laughed.

Davy cocked his right arm and was set to spring when the couple's child cried out. Little children were often sensitive to the threat of impending violence, and the youngster was clinging to his mother while regarding the warriors and Davy with troubled eyes.

It gave Davy pause. If he fought tooth and nail to keep from having those irons slapped on, some damage was bound to be done to the couple's possessions. Maybe the couple or their child would be hurt.

Davy could not allow that, not after all the kindness they had shown him. Against his better judgment, his innards churning in turmoil, he slowly straightened and held out his arms. "Get it over with, vermin," he said.

Surly Face did not waste a second. At a curt nod from him, the other three warriors seized Davy and bore him roughly to the ground. Surly Face leaned over Davy's legs, not his wrists. There was a loud click. Then another. Stepping back, Surly

Face nodded and made a comment that struck his three companions as funny. Clapping one another on the back, they filed from the lodge.

Davy rose on his elbows. The irons encircled his legs above the ankles, linked by the rusty chain, which, only a foot and a half long, did not allow for much freedom of movement. Davy lifted both legs, the chain clattering.

White-Hollow-Horn stared sadly down at the shackles. "I am sorry," he signed.

"Not half as sorry as me," Davy responded aloud while signing, "Thank you." Sitting up, he examined both shackles. They were as old as the hills, the locks as rusty as, if not rustier than, the chain.

Brought over on the *Mayflower*, he thought in jest, trying to cheer himself up. It did not work.

White-Hollow-Horn's wife offered Davy some broth, but he shook his head and flopped onto his back. He had no appetite. Who could blame him, when everything that could go wrong *had* gone wrong?

The couple left him alone for over an hour. Davy tried to doze off to spare himself the misery of contemplating what lay in store for him, but he was too upset.

His curiosity grew when White-Hollow-Horn collected an armful of belongings and brought them over. Sitting cross-legged, the young warrior proceeded to place the objects in front of him and explain the sign equivalent of each.

Davy motioned to be left alone. His spirits had sunk to a rare low, and he would rather just lie there and mope. It was ridiculous to expect him to apply himself in his current frame of mind.

But White-Hollow-Horn ignored him. Nudging his leg, the young Sioux pointed at a bone sewing needle and made a hand sign. He repeated it over

and over until Davy gave in and imitated him.
Next the warrior taught him the sign for "dress"
and "belt" and "hair."

Davy's resistance melted. It was better to be doing something—anything—than to lie there pouting. His pa had always criticized them sternly
whenever they started to feel sorry for themselves.
"Moping is for those with weak dispositions,"
John Crockett had been wont to say. "Anyone with
grit never complains about their lot in life. They
go out and improve it if it isn't to their liking."

The couple took turns instructing him. Willow
Woman, White-Hollow-Horn's wife, was even
more adept at it than her husband. She had a flair
for teaching and would have made an excellent
schoolmarm.

It was close to midnight, by Davy's reckoning,
when his hosts saw fit to quit. Their boy was sound
asleep by then. They spread out a heavy buffalo
hide beside him and were soon in dreamland
themselves.

For Davy, sleep was elusive. He tossed. He
turned. His mind was plagued by images of Flavius in dire peril, and by bittersweet recollections
of his wife and children. It seemed that this time
he had bitten off more than he could chew, as the
saying went.

He had gone on one gallivant too many.

Morning dawned brisk and clear. Davy was es-
corted to the river to wash. It took a while for him
to get the hang of moving around with the leg
irons on. They were an extremely heavy, cumber-
some affair. Each leg felt as if it weighed a ton,
and he could not take a full stride for fear that the
chain would jerk him off balance. A slow, sham-
bling stride was best.

Some of the Sioux saw him. He noticed that quite a few did not appear pleased that he was in shackles. Maybe it went against their grain. Indians everywhere valued their freedom as highly as their lives. In the estimation of the Sioux, it was probably better to slay their enemies outright than to humiliate them.

His education in sign resumed after the morning meal. Willow Woman took the first shift, her husband the second. Once every article in the lodge had been named, they took him outdoors again, pointing out anything and everything. He grew concerned that they were trying to teach him too much, too fast. At the rate it was going, he'd forget half the gestures they had taught him by sunset.

But the pace slowed considerably after a short break at noon. The couple had run out of objects and commenced with abstract signs that had to do with ideas and values and such, things like anger, love, grief and happiness.

Davy surprised himself. He learned the symbols much more readily than he would have imagined, and he did not forget what he had learned as he fretted he would.

The next day involved more of the same. By late afternoon he was able to hold a basic conversation on just about any subject.

He made it his first order of business to learn as much as he could about his captors. That they called themselves the Dakotas he already knew. That they were further divided into seven or more subtribes, he did not. The band he was with called themselves *Tetons* as much as anything else, so he took to referring to them by that name as well.

The Sioux were a powerful people. Their combined tribes controlled an enormous territory that stretched from east of the Missouri River, north to what they called the Greasy Grass River, and west to what were known as the Black Hills.

White-Hollow-Horn mentioned that his people had few dealings with the whites, which sparked Davy to ask a few questions. In order to pose one, a person first had to hold their right hand palm out at shoulder height, with the fingers extended, then rotate the hand slightly two or three times, using the wrist alone.

"Where did the tin cup your wife has come from?"

The young warrior averted his eyes. "From a white trapper who tried to pass through our country to the mountains."

Davy did not need to ask what had happened to the trapper. "And these?" he inquired, tapping the iron on his left leg.

"They were given to us by a man unlike any we ever saw. His skin was the color of night and his hair was short and curly," White-Hollow-Horn signed.

A black man? Davy speculated. Maybe a runaway slave.

"He came from the rising sun," White-Hollow-Horn signed. "He was fleeing from bad white men who made him live where he did not want to live and to do work that he did not want to do." He paused. "This was before my time. My grandfather and others saw him and have never forgotten."

"Was he killed too?" Davy bluntly asked.

"No," White-Hollow-Horn said. "We wanted him to stay with us, but he went on. Later we heard that he shared a pipe with the Crows and stayed with them." The young warrior snorted. "It upset my grandfather. He never could understand how anyone could pick the *Crows* over us."

"Have any other white or black men visited you?"

"Twice. One time a man we called Peacemaker came to us and offered to make peace between us and the Pawnees and other tribes. We told him that the Pawnees were not to be trusted, that they would kill him if he went into their country, but he would not listen. He went, and we never heard of him again."

"And the other time?"

"Many men came down the river in boats," the young warrior revealed. "They smoked with us and gave us steel knives and tobacco and bells. Our chief at the time was given a flag, which has been passed from chief to chief since. Black Buffalo has it now."

Davy recalled hearing that Lewis and Clark had made it a point to pass out flags on their historic journey, and he could not help but wonder if he had fallen in with one of the tribes visited by that famous pair.

White-Hollow-Horn frowned. "I want you to know I would not have taken you captive, Tail Hat—"

"Tail Hat?" Davy signed quizzically.

The warrior nodded. "That is what my people call you. No one has ever seen a white man wear a hat like yours." He glanced at the coonskin cap and chuckled, then became serious again. "As I was saying, I was content to let you go your way in peace. You did not try to shoot me when you could have. But Struck-By-Blackfeet and Half Man did not agree. That is why Half Man grabbed your gun."

At last Davy had learned the name of the warrior who had been shot, as well as the scarred one who was making his life so miserable. "I hope Black

Buffalo will listen to reason. The shooting was an accident."

"I have said as much," White-Hollow-Horn signed. "But Struck-By-Blackfeet says that you shot Half Man on purpose. In two sleeps the council will decide who to believe."

"I can hardly wait," Davy said to himself. To the Teton, he signed, "I do not need to ask what will happen if they side with Struck-By-Blackfeet. But what if they believe you and me? Will Black Buffalo open these and let me go free?" He tapped the leg irons again.

White-Hollow-Horn glanced at the shackles, then at Davy, then back again. "They can be opened?"

"With a—" Davy began to sign, but stopped because he had not been taught the sign, if there was one, for a key. So he said it out loud and motioned as if unlocking one of the irons.

The warrior was more perplexed than ever. "I have never heard of what you say," he responded. "The black man did not give us one."

Chapter Six

Flavius Harris had never seen a grizzly bear up close before. He'd heard all the tall tales that made the rounds of the taverns in Tennessee, though.

Grizzlies were supposed to be monsters twice the size of the biggest black bear that ever lived. Silver-tips, as some called them, were said to have claws five inches long that could shear through flesh and bone as if they were butter. They said it sometimes took ten or twenty shots to bring a single grizzly down, and even then it took hours or days for the bear to expire. And grizzlies would go out of their way to hunt down and kill any human brash enough to be caught in their territory.

Flavius had dismissed most of the talk as idle tavern gossip. When men had a few stiff drinks under the belt, it was natural for them to swap stories to see who could outdo the other. Davy was the acknowledged king in that regard in middle and western Tennessee. No one could match the whoppers he told. Why, if there were ever a national Tall Tale Contest, Davy Crockett would win hands down.

With respect to silver-tips, however, it turned out that the reports had not been greatly exaggerated at all. In fact, if anything, they did not do the bears justice.

For coming down the game trail toward Flavius was a bear fit to give the bravest man nightmares. It was enormous. No, it was bigger than enormous. The head was as broad and thick as a tree stump, the body nearly as massive as a bull buffalo's.

It was so fantastic that Flavius reined up in amazement and gawked.

The silver-tip shambled lower, its nose close to the ground, sniffing loudly. It had a ponderous yet oddly light tread for a creature endowed with legs as big around as molasses barrels. Gigantic muscles rippled beneath its lustrous coat. Adding to its monstrous proportions was a pronounced hump on its shoulders.

So astonished was Flavius that he gave no thought to the danger he was in. Not until the bear lifted its head and saw him did he realize that to sit there admiring its size might not be the smartest thing in the world to do. Prudence dictated he light a rag before the bear decided he'd make a dandy meal.

The grizzly grunted. Halting, it sniffed the air.

Flavius hesitated. Any movement might provoke an attack. Maybe if he pretended he was a rock the bear would go its merry way. Maybe it had a full belly and was not interested in eating at the moment. Maybe the stories about their ferocity had been overblown a mite.

For tense seconds the tableau was frozen. Then,

flabbergasting Flavius, the grizzly started to back up. He smiled, thinking that the worst was over, that he had met the holy terror of the wilderness and lived to tell about it. His luck was changing for the better.

The dun had to prove him wrong. Whinnying, it shied, stomping its hooves.

As if fired from a catapult, the silver-tip hurtled toward them. There was no warning growl, no display of temper. It simply dug in its claws and attacked. Jaws that could crush bone like paper gaped wide.

Flavius reined the horse around and fled. He did not even try to get off a shot. The ball was as apt to glance off the bear's skull as penetrate, and going for a lung or heart shot was an iffy proposition under the best of circumstances.

Too late, Flavius remembered Little Hickory. He glanced around to see the grizzly moving with remarkable alacrity for something its size. The calf stood a few yards to the left of the trail, close to the vegetation, staring after the dun.

Don't move! Flavius mentally screamed. So long as the bear did not notice it, the calf would be safe. "Chase me!" he shouted, recollecting that over short distances a silver-tip could rival a horse in speed.

The monster shot into the basin, a booming growl issuing from its curled lips.

"Slowpoke!" Flavius gave the dun a whack with the stock of his rifle. "You couldn't catch a turtle!" His bluster withered when the bear put on a burst of speed that cut the gap by a third. At the rate it was moving, it would overtake him in seconds.

Little Hickory did not have brains enough to stay put or to hide. The calf followed them, bawling loudly.

The cry brought the grizzly to a sliding stop. Partially turning, it saw Little Hickory.

In fear for the calf's life, Flavius hauled on the reins and turned back toward the bear. He had gone to too much trouble on the little buffalo's behalf to stand idly by while the silver-tip devoured it. Thirty feet from the colossus, he cut the dun broadside and wedged his rifle to his shoulder.

Little Hickory had also stopped. The calf regarded the grizzly without a hint of fright. It bawled again, but this time the cry held a new note, more a challenge than a whimper. Lowering its stubby horns, it pawed at the ground, first one front hoof, then the other.

Flavius could not believe his eyes. The plucky calf was fixing to charge! A snowflake would have a better chance in a blacksmith's furnace than the young buffalo had against a bear that size. "No!" he hollered. "Stay where you are!"

Little Hickory paid no heed. Moving slowly forward, he stomped some more, snorting in perfect imitation of a full-grown bull.

The grizzly acted more confused than anything. It stared at the calf, then at Flavius and the dun. Snarling, it lumbered toward Little Hickory, stopping when the calf tossed its head and bawled another challenge.

Flavius centered the front bead on the bear's chest and kneed his mount closer. The moment it went after the calf, he would fire. Perhaps the sound and the pain would make it come after him instead.

The bear suddenly reared onto two legs. A full eight and a half feet from the tip of its nose to the soles of its feet, it was a living mountain.

The sight filled Flavius with sheer dread. He did

not go any nearer. Little Hickory, however, did, stomping and snorting, a flea threatening a dragon.

Of all the astounding events that had occurred during the gallivant, none so bewildered and thrilled Flavius as what the bear did next. After glancing at him and at the calf, it dropped onto all fours, spun, and hastened to the west, not looking back once until it ascended the slope to the basin crest. Briefly silhouetted against the azure sky, the enormous bear woofed like a dog, then disappeared.

"Well, I'll be!" Flavius declared, at a total loss to explain why the creature had run off.

Little Hickory came over, prancing and snorting as if celebrating a victory.

Shaking his head in amusement, Flavius said, "You have more luck than sense, you dumb critter! That bear could have licked you without hardly lifting a claw."

He hated to admit it, but he was growing more attached to the animal with every hour. It wouldn't do, since before long he intended to return it to the herd it came from so it could find its mother.

"You're a caution!" Flavius said, leading the calf northwest in case the silver-tip took it into its head to return. Their luck would not hold a second time.

Somewhere, Flavius had heard that grizzlies sometimes traveled in pairs. If true, the other bear might be lurking in the brush or on the north rim, waiting in ambush.

As agitated as a fox caught in a henhouse, Flavius walked the dun up the trail, the growth hemming him in on either side. His skin prickled. Every shadow was a silver-tip about to pounce, every sound a harbinger of an attack. His relief on gaining the prairie without mishap knew no bounds.

The calf was in fine spirits. Now and again it danced off a dozen yards or so to scamper playfully about.

Flavius grew melancholy. It was all well and good to want to see the little fellow safely reunited with its mother. But his first priority should be to find Davy, and the farther he went, the less likely that was to take place.

No two ways about it. He was downright foolish. Yet when he grasped the reins firmly and prepared to leave, he could not bring himself to abandon the calf.

The sad truth was that he happened to be too damned tenderhearted for his own good. Always had been. Likely as not, he always would be.

The morning passed uneventfully, which suited Flavius just fine. By noon the temperature had climbed into the eighties and he was thirsty enough to drink a river.

Little Hickory, tired of acting the fool, walked along with his head low.

Locating water was crucial. As thirsty as Flavius was, the dun was much worse off. The horse had not had a drink in more than two days.

If he lost his mount, he might as well stick the muzzle of a pistol in his mouth and squeeze the trigger. He could no more survive afoot than a fish could out of water.

As glum as a pallbearer, Flavius brooded the whole afternoon. Had Davy been there, he would have scolded Flavius for being too full of himself.

"Always look at the bright side," Davy remarked whenever Flavius was in the doldrums. "Things are never as bad as they seem."

Which was fine for the brawny Irishman to say. Davy was not a fretter by nature.

Flavius was, and he would be the first to admit it. Ever since he could recall, he had been one to grow depressed when things did not go the way they should. Whereas hardships and setbacks only challenged Davy to overcome them, Flavius was more prone to whine and pout over the bad hand fate dealt him.

That night he pouted plenty. They had gone over ten miles and not seen a lick of water. Nor had he found any tracks belonging to a shod horse.

It was too depressing for words. Flavius slept little that night, arising before first light to be on his way. The morning was as uneventful as the previous afternoon. Horse and buffalo had lost most of their vitality, plodding along on weary legs.

But then the dun nickered, its gait increasing. Flavius looked up and spied a long line of trees running from north to south. "It's the river!" he exclaimed.

Whether it was the Missouri or the Mississippi was irrelevant. Flavius could not wait to dip his face into the cool, invigorating water and gulp to his heart's content. Spurring the dun into a trot, he was so elated that he did not notice tendrils of smoke curling toward the clouds until he had gone another quarter of a mile.

Flavius marked the position and angled well to the north of it. Few whites ever visited that region, so the makers of that fire had to be Indians. No doubt unfriendly Indians.

Little Hickory had caught the scent of water and was still hurrying due east.

"Where do you think you're going?" Flavius said. "Do you want to end up as a mess of steaks?"

Having once worked for a short spell as a drover, he used his experience with cattle to swing wide in front of the buffalo and steer it northward. Stubbornly, the calf balked, trying again and again to slip past the dun.

"Uppity cuss," Flavius grumbled. "Scare off one measly grizzly and you start acting too big for your britches." He cut to the left and prevented Little Hickory from getting around him. "I'm doing this for your own good, you know."

It took some doing, but at length Flavius had the calf going in the direction he desired. Vigilant, he approached the willows and briars that lined the shore, and dismounted just before he entered.

Flavius would have left the horse and the buffalo there and gone to investigate, but neither animal could be counted on to wait patiently when they were so thirsty. Leading the dun by the reins, he cautiously moved toward the river. Little Hickory walked at his side, head high, nostrils flaring. The buffalo, with that invaluable sixth sense that all wild things possess, knew that something was amiss, too.

The wide waterway was a winding snake, twisting and turning in a shallow channel that had been carved from bottomlands ages past.

Flavius scouted both sides before breaking cover. There was a bend forty yards away on the right, another sixty yards off on the left. Other than a pair of whitetail does on the opposite shore, he had that stretch of the river all to himself. The smoke was half a mile to the south, so he deemed it safe.

Tugging on the reins, the dun waded into the river and buried its muzzle. Little Hickory drank a surprisingly small amount, then gamboled about, splashing water every which way.

Flavius bent over facing the willows so no one could sneak up on him while he drank. He lowered both hands. He disregarded a loud splash behind him. It was only the calf, enjoying itself.

Without warning, pain exploded as something slammed into his backside. Flung forward, Flavius stumbled and almost fell headfirst into the river. He had to pump his legs to keep his balance, clasping the rifle to him so it would not drop. As soon as he regained his footing, he stopped and whirled.

At first Flavius assumed he had been shot, but he had not heard a gun. No war whoops rang out, either. If there were hostiles across the river, they were lying low.

He clutched his bottom, seeking evidence of blood. Had it been an arrow? A rock?

No.

It had been a buffalo.

Little Hickory stood nearby, head held low, about to charge. The calf snorted and huffed like a grown bull about to clash with a rival.

"You butted me?" Flavius declared, too sore to think it funny. "Why, you sawed-off runt! I ought to kick you from here to Tennessee!"

Tail high, Little Hickory spun and bounded out into knee-deep water, spraying the dun as he went by. The horse, irritated, backed away, vigorously shaking its head to get water out of its eyes.

Any other time or place and Flavius would have laughed himself silly. As it was, he opened his mouth to guffaw, then thought better of the idea. Whoever was responsible for the smoke might be nearer than he reckoned.

After quenching his thirst, Flavius fetched the dun. Little Hickory was sporting about, as frisky as a colt. Flavius never knew that buffalo had so much playfulness in them.

Looping the reins around a low limb, he hustled back out to retrieve the calf, but Little Hickory sidestepped to avoid him, bleating like a billy goat when he grabbed at its neck.

"We've no time for this nonsense," Flavius said, worried that they would be discovered. "Now, come on." Moving slowly so as not to provoke Little Hickory into running off, he was almost near enough to touch it when the calf trotted on around him, heading to the south.

"Dang it, no!" Flavius rasped. His upset tone did not help any. Little Hickory ran farther, then paused to look at him with those great innocent eyes as if to say, "Let's play!"

Racking his brain for a means of outwitting the calf, Flavius decided to walk off and go about his business. Little Hickory was bound to tire of all the nonsense and follow him, just as the calf had been doing for the past couple of days.

Accordingly, he stepped from the river, reclaimed the dun, and threaded through the willows to a patch of high brush. He did not glance around once. So confident was he that the calf had trailed him that he ground-hitched the horse and loosened the cinch before he turned.

The buffalo was gone.

His pulse quickening, Flavius dashed to the grass bordering the river. Little Hickory was close to the southern bend. Once around it, whichever tribe was camped yonder might see him. Indians would never pass up a golden opportunity to treat themselves to all that tender meat on the hoof.

"Damn it all!" Flavius complained, giving chase. He stuck to the winding shoreline, gaining ground rapidly but not fast enough to head off the calf, which trotted around the turn well before he got there.

In order to stay hidden, Flavius moved deeper into the belt of verdant growth. Slipping westward, he soon came to a tree flanked by thickets. He leaned his rifle against the bole, jumped, grasped a low limb, and pulled himself into a fork. Climbing higher, he saw Little Hickory close to shore approximately sixty feet past the bend. A short straight stretch ended at another winding turn to the southeast. Beyond it rose the smoke.

For the moment the calf was safe. How long, though, before a war party or hunting party appeared? Flavius scrambled down, scraping a shin on the trunk. In his haste he nearly forgot the rifle. He also made more noise than he liked, but it could not be helped.

Calling on all the woods lore he had learned, Flavius crept toward the spot where he had seen Little Hickory. The ornery calf's antics were enough to plague a saint. It was worse than having a kid to watch after.

A low rise allowed Flavius to survey the straight stretch without leaving cover. Little Hickory was on land now, grazing on sweet short grass. Flavius tried to crawl close enough to grab the hairy hellion, but as he began to slide over the rise an object appeared on a bend in the river.

Flavius pressed his body as flat as a snake's, scarcely breathing. A canoe glided smoothly upriver, a hefty man at each end manning paddles, two more at ease in the center. Judging by their dress and their long hair, he pegged them as Indians. But as the distance narrowed, it was apparent that he was wrong.

They were white men!

Overwhelmed by pure joy, Flavius watched the

canoe knife the surface. His ordeal was over! He'd explain his plight to these men and they would help him get back to civilization safely. Within a month he'd be sitting on the rocking chair on the front porch of his cabin savoring Matilda's raspberry tea.

Flavius was about to leap up and screech like a banshee to catch their attention when one of the men in the center of the canoe raised a long rifle and took deliberate aim at Little Hickory.

The calf had spied the quartet but went on grazing as if nothing out of the ordinary were taking place. Thanks to the time it had spent with Flavius, it displayed no fear of man. Munching hungrily, the unsuspecting little buffalo was an ideal target.

Flavius was outraged. It wasn't fitting for any hunter to shoot a helpless young critter like Little Hickory unless the hunter was on the verge of starving to death.

The man taking aim stopped when the frontiersman behind him placed a restraining hand on his shoulder. They exchanged words and the first man reluctantly lowered his gun.

The crisis past, Flavius coiled his legs under him to stand. Just then the canoe drew close enough for him to see the men even more clearly and to hear their next words.

"So what if any stinkin' Injuns hear," the man who had been going to shoot the calf said. "I ain't afeared of them boys."

"We're mighty tired of hearin' how brave you are, Clem," said the man who had stopped him. "But that's only 'cause you aren't smart enough to be scared. The rest of us know enough not to put our lives at risk without good cause."

Clem bristled. "Watch your tongue, Gallows. I

84

don't let anyone insult me."

The burly man in the bow of the canoe stopped paddling and twisted to scowl at the pair. He was a swarthy, greasy specimen, who looked as if he had not taken a bath in a coon's age. "That's enough out of the both of you," he snarled. "I'm sick and tired of listening to you bicker. You're worse than those rotten squaws!"

From the stern of the canoe rose gruff laughter. "Hellfire, Shaw! You know how damn crotchety Clem gets when he hasn't killed anyone in a spell." The man laughed some more. "I swear, he's more bloodthirsty than the Blackfeet and Comanches combined. Remember the time he strangled that old trapper just to see him squirm?"

Flavius did not stand up, even though the canoe was drawing abreast of Little Hickory. An uneasy feeling deep in the pit of his stomach rooted him where he was. Any men who could joke about murdering someone were not the sorts whose acquaintance he was anxious to make.

The canoe floated on around the bend to the north. Flavius did not waste another second. Dashing to the calf, he shooed it toward the low rise. He was surprised to glimpse smoke still curling above the willows. Had those four been careless enough to move on without putting their fire out? Or were there more in their party?

In answer, from the vicinity of the smoke came a woman's piercing scream.

Chapter Seven

Davy Crockett was in a rare funk.

As if it were not bad enough that he had been taken captive by the Teton Dakotas and slapped into leg irons older than he was, he now faced the bleak likelihood of being unable to get them off, ever.

The next morning Davy persuaded White-Hollow-Horn to go to Black Buffalo and inquire about the missing key. He learned that none of the Sioux had ever seen one.

Davy did not take the news well. Escaping would be hard enough without being burdened by the irons. Angrily smacking a fist against a palm, he hunkered on his bedding and glowered. His behavior disturbed the young Sioux couple.

"Question?" White-Hollow-Horn signed. "Why do your eyes burn, Tail Hat? The last man to wear those did not act like you."

"Your people put them on another white man before me?"

"No," White-Hollow-Horn answered. "He was a Blood, part of a war party that tried to steal our horses. We drove them off, killing two and taking him captive."

Davy was about to ask how they had gotten the shackles off the Blood when a commotion broke out outside. Tetons were running about, some yelling back and forth.

"I am sorry. I must go find out what is happening," White-Hollow-Horn signed. "We will talk more of this later." He hastened out.

Willow Woman offered Davy some water, but he declined. He also refused a sweetcake. She put it back into a parfleche, then sat near him. "Your heart is heavy, Tail Hat. I can understand why. Know, though, that my husband and a few others want to have you freed without harm," she signed. "Their words may prevail at the council. Do not give up hope."

"I am grateful for his help, and for the kindness you have shown me," Davy responded. "Your words are from the heart. So they cheer me a little. But we both know that Struck-By-Blackfeet and others want me dead and will not rest until I am."

Struck-By-Blackfeet's facial scar had been inflicted by a Blackfoot war club during a raid when he was a small child. His feats in battle had earned him a place on the council, but White-Hollow-Horn had revealed that Struck-By-Blackfeet was not very well liked by the majority of the Dakotas. He was too brash, too arrogant, even with his own kind.

"Figures," Davy had muttered.

The ruckus outside the lodge grew louder. Davy saw Willow Woman stiffen. "What is wrong?" he asked.

"They say that some women have been stolen,"

the young wife replied. "I did not hear their names." She cast a worried look at her son, who was playing with his round stone. "Some enemies must be nearby. The men will drive them off."

Davy had learned that warfare was an important part of the Teton way of life. Warriors rose to positions of leadership by the valor they showed in battle. They had a system set up of grading brave deeds, which White-Hollow-Horn called "counting coup."

He did not have all the particulars down pat, but it seemed that a man earned a first coup by striking a living enemy, a second coup by killing a foe without actually touching him, and so on.

Any warrior who met an enemy in personal combat was held in higher esteem than a warrior who shot from ambush. It was regarded as braver for a man to slay with a club or knife than with a bow from a safe distance.

Being wounded was also worth merit. So was rescuing a wounded Teton under enemy fire.

So ingrained was the making of war that little boys were versed in it from the moment they were old enough to stand.

Grown warriors never left camp without their weapons. Some, Davy had been told, took their favorite war horses into their lodges whenever raiders were known to be in the vicinity.

And raiders came fairly often. The Tetons, according to his hosts, at the moment were at war with eight neighboring Sioux tribes, a source of great pride to them. "The more powerful a tribe is, the more enemies they have," White-Hollow-Horn had signed. "The Crows, the Blackfeet, the Bloods, they all respect us because we are worthy enemies."

In a way, the Tetons reminded Davy of certain

officers he had met during the Creek War, men to whom glory in battle was everything. They were the ones who would gladly risk their lives to earn new medals, the ones who proudly displayed their many decorations on their uniforms.

The buffalo-hide flap parted. White-Hollow-Horn, his features grim, signed to Davy without entering. "Come with me, Tail Hat. Black Buffalo would speak to you."

"Why?" Davy asked. That he got no reply was worrisome. Shuffling into the bright sunshine, he squinted against the glare as he dogged White-Hollow-Horn's steps around the circle. The Teton chief and several other leaders were waiting for him, among them Struck-By-Blackfeet.

Davy observed another warrior off to one side, a younger man, naked except for a breechcloth, who was greedily wolfing pemmican.

Black Buffalo did not mince words. Or, in this case, sign language. "White-Hollow-Horn tells me that you can now understand me," he signed, his fingers flying.

"I can if you do not go too fast," Davy responded.

The chief pointed at Davy's scarred nemesis. "Struck-By-Blackfeet thinks that you have lied to us. He thinks that you came to our country to steal our women."

Davy found the notion preposterous, and laughed. "I have a woman of my own who would shoot me if I tried to take another."

Black Buffalo was not the least bit amused. "Maybe you and your friends steal our women to trade to others."

Davy had not mentioned Flavius, since it was all too plain that the Sioux would go hunt him down if he did. "I did not come to your country with anyone else," he fibbed.

This time Struck-By-Blackfeet replied. Stepping up, he jabbed a finger into Davy's chest, then signed, "You lie, white dog! We know the truth!" He indicated the man eating the pemmican. "Our Oglala brother from the south rode his horse to death to warn us that your people stole four women from his village and now they are on their way here to steal some Teton women."

"I am not with any other whites," Davy insisted. He could see that the rest were skeptical, except for his friend White-Hollow-Horn. "If the ones you mention stole from a village to the south, how is it that I was near your own village when you caught me?" It was a clever rebuttal, he thought, but the scarred Teton was just as clever.

Struck-By-Blackfeet sneered. "You were sent ahead to scout our village for them." Seizing Davy by the front of the shirt, he hissed like a serpent about to strike.

"Release him," Black Buffalo signed.

The scarred warrior had one hand near his knife. In contempt, he pushed Davy so hard that Davy nearly fell. "Your hair will hang from my coup stick before long, white dog," he signed viciously.

Davy came close to making a fatal mistake. Incensed, he balled his hands together and was set to wallop Struck-By-Blackfeet across the jaw, when White-Hollow-Horn stepped between them.

"There is a way to prove whether Tail Hat speaks with two tongues," he signed. "When we find these white men, we will question them to find out if they know him."

The Oglala, who had been watching closely, leaped erect and signed bitterly, "The ones who stole our women must be wiped out! We claim the right of first coup, and the right to kill them as we see fit! We must teach all whites that any who raid the Dakotas will be punished."

"Be calm, Lame Deer," Black Buffalo signed. "Have we not given our word to help your people catch them? You can do with them as you will. All we ask is that we be allowed to question them before you put them to death."

Lame Deer's wrath subsided. "It will be as you want. I am sure Long Forelock, our chief, will agree to help you."

The warriors filed out, leaving Davy alone with White-Hollow-Horn. "What next?" Davy asked.

"We leave as soon as the women have packed food for us," the young warrior answered. "Three groups will range to the south to head off these bad men before they can reach our village. You must accompany me."

Davy glanced at his ankles. How the devil did they expect him to ride with his legs shackled? He posed the question to his benefactor.

"I asked the same thing," White-Hollow-Horn signed. "Some of the men were for leaving you here. Struck-By-Blackfeet suggested we throw you over a horse on your belly." He frowned. "That is what will be done."

And so it was, much to Davy's regret. His protests were in vain. A pair of sturdy specimens hoisted him by the arms and legs onto a lively pinto, then tied his wrists to his ankles so he would not slip off. It was terribly uncomfortable, more so once they headed out. He was jostled, bumped, and bruised, his stomach so sore after a while that he shifted as far as the ropes allowed onto his right side to spare him the torment.

White-Hollow-Horn personally led the pinto. They were part of a band of twenty warriors who paralleled the Missouri River. Another band crossed and roved to the east, while a third swung to the west to scour the fringe of the prairie.

It was believed that the whites were coming by canoe, but some of the Soux were of the opinion that the women stealers might cache their canoes and try to sneak up on the village from another direction.

Black Buffalo was in charge of the group that included Davy. For that Davy was glad. The high chief seemed to be the only one capable of keeping a tight rein on Struck-By-Blackfeet, whose constant glares were ample proof that he was just waiting for his chance to finish Davy off.

That evening they camped in a clearing close to the gurgling water. Davy was unceremoniously dumped beside a log and left to his own devices while the warriors tended to the horses and a fire. Several men went off to hunt, returning with a fine buck in good order.

White-Hollow-Horn brought Davy a portion on a makeshift plate of bark. "It is all that is left," he signed apologetically as he perched on the log.

Famished enough to eat a bear, Davy dug in with relish. It was truly paltry, but to a starved man any food is a feast. Licking his fingers clean of grease when he was done, he burped, then grinned.

"Would you like water, too?" White-Hollow-Horn signed.

"Soon," Davy said, more interested in something that had stirred his curiosity. "Tell me, friend. Why would white men steal Teton women when they can get women of their own anywhere else?"

"These men do not steal just ours," White-Hollow-Horn signed. "They have taken women from the Rees, from the Mandans, from the Crows, and others."

"How long has this been going on?"

"They have been doing it since before I was born. I remember my grandfather telling me how a cousin of his disappeared when she went to pick berries with other girls. They found the tracks of white men and horses. My grandfather and a large party chased them for many sleeps but could not catch them. He was very sad at the loss. She was a pleasure to be around."

"Why are the women stolen?"

"No one knows." White-Hollow-Horn paused. "Once, during a truce, a Ree chief told us that he had heard from a white trapper about a tribe that lives far to the south. This tribe is made up of some men who are Indian, some men who are white, and some men who are half of both. They buy and sell women of all kinds."

Unreliable hearsay, Davy reckoned. He had never heard of any tribe fitting that description, and with all the stories bandied about concerning the frontier, he was sure that he would have if the tribe really existed.

Yet there was no denying that the whites who had been taking women were making life doubly hazardous for innocent traders and trappers who might come along after them. Like Davy, they would be branded guilty simply because they were of the same race.

The Sioux did not do anything halfway. When they were at war with a tribe, they were at war with the *entire* tribe, not just a band or two. The same would apply if they formally went on the warpath against the women-stealers. Because the culprits were white, the Sioux would make war on *all* whites.

Davy signed, "Question. What will happen if these men admit that they do not know me? Will I be spared?"

The young Teton stared toward the fire, where Struck-By-Blackfeet sat. "I cannot say, Tail Hat. I would set you free, but I am not the one who will decide. Perhaps you will be taken back and brought before the council again."

"I wish I may be shot if I let that happen," Davy said aloud to himself. Something told him that if he ever set foot in their village again, he would never leave it. Popular sentiment would be against him this time, especially if the stolen Oglalas were not rescued.

"This is hard for you, I know," White-Hollow-Horn signed. "But you must not lose your temper as you almost did earlier. Should you hit Struck-By-Blackfeet or any other warrior, they can kill you. I will not be able to interfere."

Davy made a mental note not to forget the advice. He cast the piece of bark aside, and in doing so his shackles rattled. It reminded him of the comment the young warrior had made that morning. "You mentioned a Blood warrior who wore these," he signed, rattling them again.

"Mad Wolf. Yes. He was hurt by an arrow while trying to run off six horses. We removed the arrow and tied him to a stake. Some were worried he would bite through the rope in the night, so those were brought and put on him."

"How did you free him when the time came?"

"We did not. He freed himself and escaped. Later we heard from the Cheyennes that the Bloods had a great laugh at our expense over how cleverly Mad Wolf tricked us."

Davy examined the irons with renewed interest. How had a man who had never seen the contraptions before managed to get shut of them? "Where was Mad Wolf when this happened?"

"Near the river," White-Hollow-Horn said. "He had been taken there to wash his wound. The men who were picked to watch him turned their backs for just a few moments. When next they looked, they found those lying in the grass."

There was so much rust that flakes rubbed off at the merest touch. Davy ran his fingers over the right shackle, which otherwise was undamaged. He found no hidden buttons or any other means of opening the lock. "Was there blood?" he inquired. Since no other way presented itself, he guessed that the Blood warrior must have had exceptionally thin legs and been able to slide his feet out, scraping his skin raw in the process.

"None," White-Hollow-Horn answered, deflating his theory. "We believe he had powerful medicine to open them like he did."

The warrior went to join the circle around the campfire, leaving Davy alone in the gathering gloom. Evidently the Tetons did not rate his medicine as high as the Blood's; none bothered to stand guard over him.

Davy studied the string of horses. Tethered among them was his sorrel, which had been appropriated by none other than Struck-By-Blackfeet. So had his rifle and tomahawk.

The family of the man Davy had accidentally shot had laid claim to Davy's pistols, while another warrior who had been on the buffalo hunt and had ridden up shortly after Davy had been knocked out wound up with Davy's knife.

The last item could easily be replaced once Davy reached a trading post. A new pair of pistols would cost a pretty penny, however, as would a rifle.

His tomahawk had been a gift from a Creek warrior he befriended in the Creek War. Superbly balanced, and as keen as a razor, it was one of Davy's most valued possessions.

Davy positioned himself with his back to the log and folded his arms. No one had thought to provide him with a blanket, so he was in for a long, chilly night. Resting his chin on his chest, he contemplated the fix he was in, and before he knew it, he was sound asleep.

The feeling of being touched snapped Davy awake. He was surprised to see that the fire had burned low and most of the warriors were spread out, slumbering. White-Hollow-Horn stood over him adjusting a Hudson's Bay blanket.

"I brought an extra," the Sioux signed. Smiling, he moved to a cluster of Tetons who were still awake. Included in the group was Struck-By-Blackfeet.

Davy rolled onto his left side to make himself more comfortable. His feet, weighted by the heavy chain, became entangled. He tried to separate them, but the chain had snagged under his bottom moccasin.

Sighing in exasperation, Davy brought his knees up to his chest and lowered his arms. He quickly disentangled the loop, then placed the chain beside his legs. His hand happened to brush the shackle on his left ankle. For no real reason other than petty spite, he gripped the metal loop where it was chafing his skin, and yanked.

Something clicked.

Davy felt the lock swing open and was so excited that he nearly gave himself away by partially throwing the blanket off him so he could see better. His sudden movement drew the interest of Struck-By-Blackfeet.

To fool the scarred warrior, Davy made a show

of shifting onto his back and then onto his side again, hoping to give the impression that he was having trouble getting to sleep, and that was all. Pulling the blanket as high as his chin, he feigned closing his eyes but actually left them open a crack.

Struck-By-Blackfeet stared a bit longer, then became embroiled in a conversation with one of the others.

Davy's mind was racing. All this time, and not once had he thought to give the leg irons a good, solid pull to verify that they were locked. He had taken it for granted they were, when, in fact, they were so rusted that the locks no longer worked properly. He took hold of the shackle on his right ankle, hunched his shoulders, and snapped his wrists outward. Nothing happened. Dreading that only the one would open, Davy tried again. And again. Yet a fourth time. The shackle resisted his every effort.

He had to be careful not to move about when he exerted himself or Struck-By-Blackfeet might notice and come over to investigate.

Easing onto his right side to obtain better leverage, Davy wedged the fingers of both hands under the metal loop, tensed, and pushed with all his might. A muffled grating noise, like the scraping of a nail on metal, inspired him to keep on pushing even though his fingers hurt abominably and his face was growing beet red from the strain. He would not give up now! Not when he was so close!

The second leg iron parted so abruptly that Davy lurched forward, his hands slipping off and thudding the earth. His joy at having the constraints off was short-lived. For when he glanced at the fire, Struck-By-Blackfeet had risen and was heading toward him.

Davy snored lightly, feigning sleep. The scarred Teton slowly approached, circling to get behind him. It prompted Davy to wonder if the warrior had seen something suspicious, or if he had a more sinister reason for sneaking over.

Muttering, Davy rolled onto his back. Now he could see that the warrior had halted and partly drawn his long knife. Struck-By-Blackfeet's countenance was a study in baffled hatred and blood lust. He yearned to kill Davy so badly that the arm gripping the knife shook slightly.

Davy saw the Dakota lean toward him. In another moment the deed would be done. Crying out might give Struck-By-Blackfeet pause. It also might incite the warrior to spear the blade into his body before anyone could interfere. Yet he could not just lie there. Davy compromised. Opening his eyes, he stared right at the other man.

Struck-By-Blackfeet froze, uncertainty erasing the hatred. He had the knife almost out. Another inch or so and it would be clear of the scabbard. His dark eyes darted at the men seated close to the fire. Gradually, the knife was lowered, the hand raised.

"You are as good as dead, white man," Struck-By-Blackfeet signed. "Do you know that?"

Davy did not respond.

"You think that your friend White-Hollow-Horn will convince my people to let you go. But I tell you now that my word counts for more than his, and I will see your belly slit wide and your guts spill out." Then the Dakota stomped off.

Davy drew the blanket up to his cheek and lay still as the fire dwindled. One by one the last of the warriors turned in. Tiny fingers of flame were all that lit the clearing when he rose onto his knees, draping the blanket over his shoulders as some of the Indians had done. On cat's feet he stalked toward his tormentor.

The time had come to take the bit in his teeth and make himself scarce in those parts, or die trying.

Chapter Eight

Davy Crockett had a reputation for being one of the finest hunters in all of Tennessee. His skill, everyone said, was on a par with that of the Indians.

Now was his chance to prove it. A single misstep and the Sioux would be on him like riled bees on a bear. Of the entire war party, only White-Hollow-Horn and possibly Black Buffalo had any interest in keeping him alive.

The camp was so quiet that the crackling of the embers was loud by comparison.

Tiptoeing past the outer ring of sleepers, Davy crept toward Struck-By-Blackfeet. It was lunacy, he knew, but he was not leaving without his rifle and his tomahawk.

Not all that long ago, Davy had been captured by a Fox band and escaped in the middle of the night, just like now, and the experience had taught him valuable lessons. For one thing, he'd learned never to walk between a sleeper and the fire if he could help it. For some reason, even if the man was snoring loud enough to rouse the dead, it was apt to wake him up.

For another, Davy had discovered that it was unwise to put his foot down within six inches of a sleeper's ear. No matter how quietly he did it, sometimes the faint stirring of air was enough to interrupt the man's slumber.

Accordingly, Davy methodically picked his way closer to the center of the band, where Struck-By-Blackfeet slept. The Teton had placed the rifle, ammo pouch, and powder horn beside him, but the tomahawk was wedged under the top of his breechclout.

It was to Davy's advantage that the Sioux had not posted a guard. Indians rarely did, except when they were certain enemies were close by.

It had surprised Davy to find out that most tribes did not even bother to post sentries around their villages at night. It was a tactical weakness other tribes always exploited by attacking at first light to cause the most confusion.

The same flaw had worked to the benefit of the whites during the Creek War. Time and again, they had completely surrounded unsuspecting Creek towns and either wiped them out or taken the inhabitants prisoner. Time and again, the Creeks had failed to learn by their mistake.

Now, treading carefully past a stout Sioux who rumbled like a thundercloud, Davy felt something under his sole, something that started to bend under the pressure of his weight. Instantly lifting his foot, he saw a thick twig that would have snapped like a gunshot and given him away.

The low flames cast a feeble glow over the nearest warriors. Otherwise, shadows shrouded the camp, which protected Davy seconds later when he skirted the stout Dakota and suddenly the man stopped snoring and opened his eyes.

With the blanket pulled up over his head as if to ward off the chill, Davy could pass for a warrior if he were not given a close scrutiny. So rather than stand there flat-footed, he walked on toward the fire, shuffling wearily as might a man who had just woken up.

The ruse worked. The stout Sioux smacked his lips a few times, rolled over, sighed, and was fast asleep in moments.

Davy went around three more men. Finally he was behind Struck-By-Blackfeet, who was facing the fire on his left side. Hunkering, Davy slowly reached across the warrior and reclaimed Liz, which he propped against his leg.

Retrieving the ammo pouch and powder horn required greater care. Both had long leather straps and were liable to bump against Struck-By-Blackfeet if not held just right. He lifted each as if they were fragile eggshells.

Next came the tomahawk. Davy lightly grasped the head to slide it out, but when he did, Struck-By-Blackfeet muttered in his sleep and turned partway. Davy jerked his hand back before the warrior could brush against it.

A new problem presented itself. The Teton's elbow had shifted and was covering the top half of the tomahawk.

Davy dared not touch it again until the elbow moved. But he could not squat there half the night waiting for that to happen. So either he left it there or he took a calculated gamble.

Plucking a blade of grass, Davy leaned closer and ever so delicately ran the tip across Struck-By-Blackfeet's neck. The warrior fidgeted but did not move his elbow, so Davy lightly slid the tip along the Teton's jaw.

Struck-By-Blackfeet moved his legs a few inches, but not his arms.

Every moment wasted was precious. Davy scanned the rest of the war party to confirm that none had stirred. Then he brushed the grass against Struck-By-Blackfeet's ear. It got a reaction, but not exactly the one he had bargained on.

Struck-By-Blackfeet rolled onto his stomach, turned his head toward the fire—and opened his eyes.

Davy had no forewarning, no chance to draw his arm back or to flatten.

The Sioux's brow knit. He blinked a few times. Yawning, he scratched himself, then his eyes began to close again.

It must have been intuition that made Struck-By-Blackfeet aware that someone was beside him. Davy did not make a sound. But the next moment the warrior tensed, pushed onto his elbows, and swiveled.

His arm a blur, Davy snatched his tomahawk out, whipped it on high, and brought it crashing down against the Teton's hard skull with brutal force. Struck-By-Blackfeet's eyes had started to widen, his mouth to open. The blow rendered him senseless, and he collapsed without uttering an outcry.

None of the other Sioux had budged.

Davy did not linger. Sticking the tomahawk under his belt, he slid the ammo pouch over his left arm, the powder horn over his right, and hustled to the string.

Thanks to the blanket White-Hollow-Horn had lent him, his scent was masked. Several of the horses swung their heads around, but none whinnied. He stroked the sorrel as he stepped to the rawhide rope, which parted easily at a single slice of the tomahawk.

Davy hopped on the sorrel, patting it to keep it calm. He backed from the tether, never once taking his eyes off the Dakotas. He removed the blanket, folded it three times, and draped it over his shoulder. He aimed to take it with him, but then he recollected how poor White-Hollow-Horn and Willow Woman were. They could ill afford to lose a fine blanket that must have cost them dearly in trade. Folding it once more, he slid off the sorrel, dashed to the log, and deposited it next to the shackles where the young warrior was bound to find it.

The sorrel shook its head as Davy climbed back on. Clucking softly, he moved to the head of the rope. Scattering the horses was the sensible thing to do, but he hesitated.

White-Hollow-Horn and Willow Woman owned only two. If Davy ran the string off, White-Hollow-Horn might never recover his. The loss would be devastating. A Sioux warrior was as dependent on his horse as a blacksmith was on his forge. Without them, neither could provide for his family.

Frowning, Davy settled for getting out of there with his hide intact and melted into the willows. Heading due south, he paralleled the river as the Sioux had been doing.

The smart thing to do was locate a ford and cross. In a few days he would be well to the east, safe. In a few weeks he would be home.

There was only one catch. By riding off, Davy would never know what fate had befallen Flavius. He had to try to find him. Only when he knew for certain that his friend was dead would he light a

Sioux Slaughter

shuck for the rolling green hills and verdant valleys of Tennessee.

Davy held the sorrel to a walk until he was out of earshot of the camp. From then on he maintained a steady lope where the terrain allowed. Hour after hour he forged southward, a cacophony of night sounds attending him. The howls of wolves and the yips of coyotes hardly ever ceased. No sooner would one stop than another took up the refrain elsewhere. Panthers screamed on occasion. Owls hooted their eternal question.

All went well until an hour before sunrise. Fatigue was gnawing at Davy's mind. Lulled by the motion of the sorrel, he dozed off for short spells, staying on by sheer habit. About the third time he was startled out of sleep by a loud grunt close at hand.

The sorrel came to a stop, ears pricked toward a thicket fifty yards to the southwest. Something moved in its depths, something huge.

Davy brought up his rifle, centering the front bead on the dark shape that appeared. In the gloom he could not quite distinguish what it was. The beast helped him out by striding boldly into the open, trampling the vegetation under its massive bulk.

"Damn!" Davy said.

A grizzly as big as his cabin stood eyeing the sorrel and him as if they were just what the mammoth bear hankered after for breakfast. Sniffing like a bellows, it advanced at a brisk if ponderous gait.

A narrow strip of grass bordered the river. Davy had been using it to make better time. But since it would take him right past the grizzly, he had to find another way around. Taking to the trees would not be very bright, since logs and additional obstacles would only slow the sorrel down.

That left one option. Reining to the left, Davy plunged into the Missouri, the horse wading swiftly out until the water was as high as Davy's knees. The bear came to the edge and halted. Growling, it pawed at the water but did not enter.

"Don't care for a swim?" Davy baited it as he came abreast. "I don't blame you, old hoss. It's awful cold."

The grizzly did not appreciate his humor. Suddenly snarling, it plowed in, spraying water everywhere, and barreled toward the sorrel like a steamship toward port. The current had no more effect on it than on a mountain.

"*Hee-yah!*" Davy cried, raking his heels against the sorrel's flanks. The horse took a hop, then surged forward, tail held aloft. They were in over Davy's legs and going farther every moment.

The bear was gaining. It slanted toward them, its coat glistening with moisture, its elephantine head swinging from side to side like a horizontal pendulum.

Davy goaded the sorrel to go faster. It tried its best but the deep water slowed it down, as did the treacherous footing. Twice it slipped and nearly went under.

The grizzly did not slip. Churning the Missouri like a water-bound locomotive, it had less than fifteen yards to cover before it would be on them with raking claws and saber teeth.

Repeatedly glancing at the bear, the sorrel was growing frantic. Davy twisted and brought his rifle up. He had one shot, and that was it. Without his pistols to fall back on, he had to resort to the tomahawk if the bear got that close. Twelve feet remained. Ten feet. Davy could see the bear's feral eyes clearly, see the lips curling back to expose teeth that put a black bear's to shame. His thumb curled around the hammer. Another few moments and he would have to shoot.

What transpired next qualified as a miracle in Davy's eyes. The bear was eight feet away. A short lunge, and it would have them. At that exact moment, a large fish leaped clear of the water in a high, vaulting arc directly in front of the bruin. Its leap was so swift that if Davy had blinked, he would have missed it. Yet the grizzly swiped out a paw with lightning speed, catching the fish before it struck the surface. In a twinkling the bear's gigantic jaws had clamped shut. It stopped and chewed greedily.

Davy reined toward shore. His sole hope lay in reaching it before the bear. The sorrel seemed to realize the same thing, for it did not slow a bit until they had solid ground under them once again. Pausing only to shake itself, it responded to a flick of the reins by breaking into a gallop.

The last glimpse Davy had of the grizzly was of it chomping on the head of the fish, much as a backwoodsman would chomp on a wad of chewing tobacco.

"Too close for comfort," Davy said to himself, and promptly forgot about it.

Narrow escapes were part and parcel of a frontiersman's life. For a confirmed bear hunter, they were more so. Davy had lost count of the number of cornered black bears that turned on his hounds and him and nearly ripped them to ribbons.

One such incident was memorable only because folks in his neck of the woods still talked about it as if it were a feat out of ordinary.

It had been a moonless autumn night made darker by the roiling clouds of an approaching storm. Davy's hounds had caught the scent of a bear well before sunset and set out after it. The big black, though, heard them coming and lit a rag for the deep woods.

The sun had been down for over an hour when Davy caught up with the pack. They had the bear treed, but it was so dark that Davy could barely make it out. Sighting as best he could, he'd fired and brought his quarry crashing to the earth.

Only problem was, the bear was still alive. Rising in a fury of flying claws and snapping jaws, it had torn into the dogs, tossing them like sticks.

It was no exaggeration to say that Davy had more affection for his hounds than he did anyone or anything with the exception of his wife and kids. Time and again those dogs had risked their lives so his family would have meat on the table. They were loyal, dependable, and devoted.

So when Davy saw them being scattered like chaff in the wind, he drew his butcher knife and rushed to their aid.

In the black of the stygian night, Davy could not tell one end of the bear from the other. He slashed and thought he connected. Just then his hounds closed in again. He found himself caught in the midst of a swirling whirlwind of gnashing teeth and raking paws.

One of the animals slammed into his legs, knocking him onto his back. He'd looked up to see the bear above him, slavering jaws poised to rend.

To his rescue came the hounds, biting and nipping in a frenzy. The black had turned on them, bringing one low with a powerful blow. Then, backing off, it had retreated into a narrow cleft.

Since now only one dog could get at the bear at a time, it held them off, inflicting as many wounds as it received.

Davy regained his feet. After circling around to

the top of the cleft, he had dropped onto his belly to stab at the bear's vitals. But he could not reach from where he was. So, in order to spare his hounds from further harm, he had slipped his legs over the rim and slid to the bottom behind the bear.

It had seemed like a fine brainstorm at the time. Only now he was hemmed in by the steep earthen walls on either side and the bear in front. There was barely room to move, let alone raise an arm. Worse, he could not see past the end of his nose if his life depended on it. The cleft was pitch black.

Davy had put himself into a nice fix. He reached out tentatively to the bear, establishing where to thrust. He barely touched the animal for fear it would realize he was there. Much to his dismay, it did.

Roaring hideously, it clawed at the right side of the cleft as if berserk. Part of the bank gave way, permitting the black bear to bend far enough back to deliver blows that missed by inches. Just a little more room and it would be able to squeeze completely around and pounce.

Davy darted in close three or four times. In each instance the bear drove him back again. He came so close to sinking cold steel into its body, yet each time he had to leap to the rear or have his own body sliced open.

Apparently sensing that their master was in trouble, the hounds redoubled their assault, snapping at whatever parts of the bear were exposed. So savage was their attack that the bear forgot about Davy for the moment and concentrated on them.

It had been then or never! Davy had dropped onto his knees and ran an arm along the bear's left side. The black could not help but feel his fingers, yet it had the hounds to contend with. So long as they kept it busy, Davy had a fighting chance of doing what needed to be done.

His fingers had brushed the bear's rib cage. Probing for the bottom rib, he found it just as the beast bent nearly in half to turn and face him. Davy had stabbed up and in, the blade parting the heavy hide and the flesh underneath like a hot knife searing through butter.

The black bear had grunted. That was all. Merely grunted.

Davy had thrown himself backward before the bear could retaliate, but it never did. Like a house of cards collapsing in on itself, the black had buckled limply to lie as still as a gravestone.

For some reason Davy had never fathomed, his clash in that cleft became the talk of western Tennessee. Whenever he visited a tavern, the patrons would gather around to hear stories of his exploits. And it never failed that someone would ask to hear about "the bear in the hole," as most phrased it.

Little did anyone know that there had been dozens of similar close shaves over the years.

Small wonder he gave no more thought to the grizzly before him now.

The encounter had banished his fatigue, though, and for several hours he rode rapidly southward, pausing every so often to give the sorrel a breather.

By the middle of the morning Davy's eyes were leaden again. He was tempted to stop and rest. But in his state he'd sleep half the day away, allowing the Dakota war party to overtake him.

The warmth of the sun did not help matters much. It made him lethargic, so sluggish that when he had to duck under a low limb, he did not duck low enough and was clipped on the shoulder. Peeved by his condition, he shook his head to clear the cobwebs.

That helped for a short while, but Davy soon realized that he had to catch some sleep, or else. Before he could, he'd best ensure that the Tetons could not find him. To that end, he urged the sorrel into the Missouri to hide his tracks.

A warm breeze fanned Davy's cheek as he rounded a bend. He was about a dozen feet from shore, just far enough for the current to erase any trace of the sorrel's passage by the time the Sioux got there.

Try as he might, Davy could not stay awake. His chin dipped, his eyelids fluttered shut. He had no idea he had slept for several minutes until the sorrel nickered and he looked up to discover the stretch of river was not the same.

"Damn my bones!" Davy grumbled. He pinched himself. He slapped himself. He tried singing a rowdy tune popular in taverns. Nothing helped.

Again Davy drifted off. If he had not taken the precaution of looping the reins around his wrist, he would have wound up drenched when his mount suddenly stopped and sidestepped. Only grasping the reins saved him from falling off.

"What's gotten into—?" Davy began, his vocal cords locking when he beheld a canoe that barred his way. Four swarthy men met his stare with icy indifference. Two held paddles. Two held rifles. The biggest man casually pointed his at Davy and smirked.

"Howdy there, mister. That's a mighty fine animal you've got. Why don't you climb off it, real slow, so I won't have to blow your brains out."

Chapter Nine

Flavius Harris had been hanging around Davy Crockett too darned long.

He tried telling himself that whatever had caused the woman to scream was none of his business. On the frontier a man was expected to mind his own affairs and no one else's. But he could not shake the persistent notion that if Davy were there, Davy would go have a look-see. That happened to be how Davy was, always doing what he felt to be right.

"Why should I do the same?" Flavius complained, then tied the calf to a stump and jogged downriver toward the scream.

He heard voices before he saw them, four women and five men ringing a small fire. It struck him as odd that all the women were on their knees with their hands behind their backs, until he saw coils of rope around their wrists. Tears streaked the cheeks of the youngest, a fine figure of a maiden who was bent over in despair. The women were Indians, but he could not tell what tribe they were from.

The five men were cut from the same cloth as the four in the canoe. That is to say, they were grungy, greasy, bearded men who had been burned bronze by the sun and hardened whipcord tough by the elements.

They also had the same air about them, an air of simmering menace, of violence lurking just under the surface. They were the kind of men Flavius avoided back home, men everyone except maybe Davy would give a wide berth on the street.

As Flavius looked on, the tallest of the five, whose left eyelid hung half shut, rose and carried a small bowl to the maiden who was crying. Jabbing her with his toe to get her attention, he held out the bowl and said, "Are you ready to eat now, or do I have to get really nasty?"

A short man whose chin came to a point paused in the act of sipping coffee, and snickered. "You're wastin' your time, Grist. That filly ain't about to cooperate."

"She hasn't since the day we stole her," commented a man who appeared to be part Indian. "I say shoot her and be done with it."

Grist shook his head. "Look at how pretty she is, Jipala. She'll fetch us a hundred dollars or better, easy, down in your neck of the woods."

The short man snickered again. "Provided she lasts until we get there. We won't get a cent for her if she's half starved. You know as well as me that the folks we deal with like 'em healthy and plump, like ripe peaches."

"She'll eat, Kline," Grist vowed. "If I have to cram the food down her throat a mouthful at a time, the bitch will eat." He held the bowl in front of the maiden's face and said something in an Indian tongue Flavius had never heard.

The maiden ignored him.

Kline cackled. "See? What did I tell you? Let her starve. It would serve her right."

"Shoot her and be done with it," Jipala repeated.

Grist did neither. With a savage wrench, he twisted the woman's head so they were eye-to-eye. She did not so much as flinch. He mashed the edge of the bowl against her lips, to no effect. Furious, he set the bowl down, stormed to the fire, and squatted.

A fourth man, whose left arm seemed crippled and permanently bent at the elbow, gestured and said, "Giving up so soon? That's not like you."

"I *never* give up, Weist. You should know that." Grist carefully plucked at the unlit end of a burning brand and lifted it from the flames. "This should do nicely," he said wickedly, turning back to the woman.

Flavius divined the man's intent and half rose to go to her aid. He hunkered back down just as fast. Exposing himself would only get him killed. Whoever these men were, they would not take kindly to meddlers.

The maiden tried to scoot backward, but Grist stomped a heavy boot on her ankle, pinning her leg. She cried out, then clenched her teeth. "Think that will help?" Grist mocked her. "If so, think again."

Flavius did not want to look, but he could not turn away. He squirmed as the brand was pressed against her calf. It made a sizzling sound, like frying bacon. The maiden thrashed, tears streaming down her cheeks. When she could endure the anguish no longer, she threw back her head and screamed.

Four of the five men were highly amused.

The fifth man, whose name Flavius had not yet learned, was the only one who did not. Like Jipala, he had Indian features, with a dash of Mexican thrown in. His countenance was as inscrutable as a rock. He never smiled, never laughed, never showed any emotion. All he did was sit there with a rifle across his thighs, alertly surveying the undergrowth every now and then.

This was the most dangerous member of the bunch, Flavius concluded, a man who would slit the throat of anyone who riled him with no compunctions at all, a natural-born killer if ever there was one. Someone Flavius must avoid at all costs.

Grist stepped back and wagged the brand in front of the maiden. Again he addressed her in the unfamiliar tongue. This time she meekly sat up, placed the bowl in her lap, and began to eat.

The other three women were studies in despair.

Flavius felt extremely sorry for them, but he did not see what he could do on their behalf. He wasn't much of a fighter, and those five cutthroats were not about to give up their captives without a struggle. They'd make worm food of him in no time.

Besides, it wasn't as if he knew the women personally. They were strangers. They meant nothing to him. He could go his own way with a clear conscience.

Or could he?

Flavius looked at them again, his heartstrings tugged by their misery. If Davy were there, he would do something. But Davy was smarter and braver and stronger.

What could Flavius do alone?

Grist had just sat down and was pouring himself a cup of coffee. Kline emptied his cup, smacking his lips. Weist was rummaging in a saddlebag. Suddenly all of them glanced up, directly toward the brush that screened Flavius.

As well they should. For Little Hickory had picked that moment to let out with a bawl that could have been heard clear back in Knoxville.

Flavius dropped lower, fearful of being seen. He thought, *Please don't bawl again! Please! Please!* But the calf did, not once but twice.

"What the hell is that?" Kline wondered.

"A deer, maybe," Weist suggested.

"Idiots," Grist said. "That's a buffalo. A mighty young one, if I'm any judge." Pursing his lips, he glanced at the half-breed who never spoke. "We could use some fresh meat. What do you say, Cuchillo? Care to do the honors?" He smirked. "Jipala can go along if you want some help."

Without uttering a word, Cuchillo rose. He wore a blue woolen shirt, leggings, and a breechclout much longer than those Flavius had seen on Indians back in the States. His moccasins were unusual also in that they rose as high as his knees. In addition to the rifle, a long knife hung from his side in a plain leather sheath. Pivoting, he blended into the brush nearest the fire.

Flavius quietly backed away until he felt it safe to stand, then rose and ran for his life, his heart beating like a hammer. He was almost too scared to think straight. If Cuchillo caught him, he was a goner for sure.

Forsaking all caution, Flavius sped pell-mell through the growth. Whether he made too much noise now was unimportant. Getting to the dun and getting out of there was what counted.

Little Hickory bawled once more as Flavius hustled into the clearing. He had half a mind to leave the calf behind, but he sank onto a knee to unfasten the rope from the stump. As he rose, the short hairs at the nape of his neck prickled. He could not say how he knew, but he was no longer alone. He whirled.

Cuchillo stood between Flavius and the dun. The half-breed glanced at the calf, his forehead creasing.

"The critter is sort of my pet," Flavius said without thinking, and felt like a jackass for saying it.

Again Cuchillo looked at Little Hickory. A peculiar quirk curled the corners of his mouth. Hefting his rifle, he began to circle to the right.

Flavius automatically circled to the left. He had leaned his rifle against the stump when he untied the calf, but he still had his pistols. Making no attempt to draw, certain that if he tried he would be dead before he touched them, he waited for the half-breed to make the next move.

The man called Cuchillo came to Little Hickory and stopped. He voiced a throaty chuckle, the first sound he had made, then faced Flavius and slowly started to rise his rifle.

Flavius had no choice now. He had to do something. So, taking a deep breath, he stabbed his hands to his flintlocks. And, as he had dreaded, the cutthroat was faster. Much faster.

As if by magic, the 'breed's rifle was level, pointed at Flavius's heart. Cuchillo grinned sadistically, as if to say, "You're as good as dead."

Flavius was as rigid as steel. His eyes were on the rifle's trigger in anticipation of the shot that would end his life. Unexpectedly, behind Cuchillo, there was a rush of motion, the patter of hooves.

It was hard to say which of them was more surprised when Cuchillo was flung forward as if smashed into by a battering ram. In a sense, he had been. A shaggy, four-legged, knob-horned battering ram that had slammed into his hind end just as it had earlier into Flavius.

Cuchillo was thrown onto his hands and knees, the rifle sent flying. He landed in front of Flavius and instantly tried to push to his feet. Flavius, on pure impulse, drove his right knee into the man's jaw with a resounding crack. Cuchillo sagged, stunned but not out. Flavius remedied that by cocking his right arm and planting his fist on the cutthroat's jaw.

Soundlessly, Cuchillo dropped.

Flavius's knuckles were aching terribly. Shaking his hand, he claimed his rifle, took Cuchillo's, and climbed onto the dun. Reining northward, he fled, saying to the calf, "Come on or we're both goners!"

For once Little Hickory obeyed without misbehaving. In moments they were shielded by the trees, but Flavius did not feel safe until they had gone over a mile without any sign of pursuit. Only then did he realize there would be none. The five men did not have any horses. He recalled seeing several canoes on the shore, but no mounts. "We did it!" he exclaimed. "Will wonders never cease!"

Little Hickory bleated to hold up his end of the conversation.

Halting, Flavius shifted to check their back trail, just in case. His thoughts turned to the four women. From what little he had gathered, they were doomed to be taken south and sold. To what purpose? Would they be forced to prostitute themselves? Or was there a more sinister purpose behind their abduction?

"What do I do now?" Flavius asked aloud.

The five slavers, or whatever they were, would be on their guard from then on. It would be next to impossible for Flavius to sneak into their camp and free the captives without being caught. Yet how could he live with himself if he rode off without helping?

A moment ago he had been so happy he could crow like a rooster. Now, depressed, Flavius walked the dun to a stand of saplings and pressed into the center, where he swung down in a small open space. Little Hickory pranced up to nuzzle his leg. Grinning despite himself, Flavius petted the feisty bundle of trouble.

One thing was clear. He had to get shed of the calf before he could help the women, or it would dog his heels and make a further nuisance of itself. Tying it had proven unwise. The next time a grizzly might hear it bawling, and that would be that.

Plenty of daylight remained. Why waste it? Flavius climbed back on the dun and headed for the open prairie. He felt awfully exposed and vulnerable leaving the heavy growth. Changing direction to the southwest, he kept his eyes skinned for the calf's kin.

Little Hickory ambled merrily along, as content as a hog in mud. Within an hour, though, the steady pace took its toll and the calf flagged.

Flavius did not stop. Every few minutes he would rise in the stirrups to scour the plain. As yet he had seen deer, he had seen antelope, he had seen coyotes and more of those strange whistling rodents. He had seen a fox and a slew of rabbits, but not a single, solitary buffalo.

By early afternoon Flavius was about ready to pull out his hair. There were supposed to be millions and millions of bison roaming the grassland, so where the hell were they? Tired, he wiped his forehead with a sleeve. As he lowered his arm, black dots appeared in the distance.

"More antelope, I reckon," Flavius remarked, and snorted. Here he was, a grown man, and he had gotten into the habit of talking to a dumb calf as if it were another person. He must have marbles for brains.

The dots grew bigger, taking on definite proportions. Distinct humps and curved horns framed hairy bulks. It was a small herd of buffalo, at last! Flavius beamed like an imbecile and slowed so as not to spook them.

"There you are!"

The calf looked up at him, tail twitching.

"What are you waiting for?" Flavius demanded, pointing. "Make tracks on over and mingle with your own kind before they mosey elsewhere."

Little Hickory stayed right where he was.

"Didn't you hear me? Haven't you caught their scent yet?" Flavius licked a forefinger and held it up, only to learn that the wind was blowing from north to south. "Of course it is," he groused. "Why should anything go right for a change?"

Leery of sending them into panicked flight, Flavius approached the grazing animals with the utmost care. He was four hundred yards out before a bull on the fringe lifted its enormous head and spotted him.

Drawing rein, Flavius waited to see if the temperamental animal would charge. It must not have believed him to be a threat, because it resumed grazing.

"This is as far as I can go," he told Little Hickory. "So shoo!" Gesturing, he sought to drive the calf off, but it merely gazed at the herd, uninterested.

"What is the matter with you?" Flavius snipped. "After all I've gone through for you, you have the gall to stand there like a bump on a log?" Sliding from the saddle, Flavius gave the calf a swat on the rump. It moved a few feet, then stopped to stare at him with what he would have sworn was the saddest expression he had ever seen on an animal.

"I've got no time for this nonsense," Flavius blustered, a lump constricting his throat. He smacked it again, and when it still lingered, he hauled off and kicked it in the posterior. That did the job.

Squalling like a hungry infant, Little Hickory bounded toward the herd.

Flavius watched intently, worried that one of the bulls might see fit to challenge the calf. From out of the herd did come an adult, but not a bull. A cow, snorting excitedly, rushed to intercept Little Hickory, and when the two met they rubbed against one another, the female licking Hickory's head just as a cat would lick her kittens. For his part, Little Hickory was beside himself with the buffalo equivalent of pure glee. He gamboled around the cow, kicking up his heels in abandon.

All's well that ends well, Flavius figured. Circumstances had apparently brought him to the very herd that the calf belonged to. Mother and offspring had been reunited, so now Flavius could get on with the task he had set for himself.

There was no hurry, though. Flavius wanted to time it so that he reached the river shortly after the sun went down, and that is exactly what he did. Shrouded by twilight, he slipped into the belt of vegetation without being spotted. So far as he knew.

Never a wizard at memorizing landmarks like Davy, Flavius was unsure how far he happened to be from the camp of the slavers. As best he could calculate, he was three or four miles to the south.

Night had claimed the prairie by the time Flavius spied a pinpoint of flickering light through the trees. He'd been worried that the slavers had packed up and paddled off to parts unknown, but they were still there.

Leaving the dun concealed in some willows, Flavius moved toward the campsite. Nervous as he was, he remembered to employ all the tricks Davy had taught him. He walked on the balls of his feet instead of the soles so as to reduce the risk of stepping on twigs. He also used the terrain to its full advantage by always having something between him and the fire, such as a tree or a bush or a thicket.

As before, voices confirmed that Flavius was getting close. Crouching, he advanced at a literal crawl, stopping every few yards to listen. The women stealers were having a fine old time, joking and laughing as if they were celebrating at Flavius's favorite tavern.

Stupid of them, Flavius thought. It didn't do to advertise one's presence in the middle of hostile territory.

Soon Flavius glimpsed the four captives. They were on the side of the fire nearest the trees, their ankles bound as well as their wrists. The woman who had been tortured had her face pressed to the grass and her shoulders were quaking. The others were, if anything, more downcast than they had been the last time. Two chanted softly.

The slavers were sprawled around the fire, passing a flask from man to man. At the moment Grist was holding court, declaring loudly, "I tell you, boys, this haul will make our pockets bulge with gold and silver. We'll have enough for a month or more in New Orleans. Think of it! Living like kings! Only the best hotels! Only the finest food!"

"And the finest women," Kline threw in. "Never forget the women."

Grist chortled lustily. "How could I, when

they're my bread and butter?" he responded with a nod at the maidens. Accepting the flask, he took a healthy swallow. "Of course, I can't take all the credit. If it weren't for Shaw and his contacts south of the border, we wouldn't be doing half as well as we are."

Weist was adding dead branches to the flames. "You sell yourself short," he commented. "Your contacts with the Comanches are just as important."

"Maybe so," Grist said, "but the mangy Comanches are too damn stingy most of the time. That last woman we sold to Red Bear should have brought twice as much as she did. She was white, after all."

Flavius was shocked. They stole *white* women too? What manner of men were these that they would treat women, red or white, as if they were cows or horses? Did they have no scruples whatsoever? He crawled a few yards to the left, to a clump of tall weeds. Once the five men fell asleep, he aimed to sneak on in and cut the maidens free.

Kline was talking. "Let's just hope Shaw and the others have as much luck with the Minniconjous as we did with the Oglalas. We'd be sittin' pretty, by God."

"Next trip we should hit the Shoshones and the Crows," Weist suggested. "I favor the mountains. It's easier to shake anyone who comes after us than it is out here along this godforsaken river."

"I wouldn't fret, were I you," Grist said. "We've been doing this for how many years now? Five? And the stupid Injuns haven't caught on yet."

Kline laughed and slapped his thigh. "I know. Ain't it glorious! We take their women and they always blame it on a neighboring tribe."

"No one's luck holds forever," Weist said, break-

David Thompson

ing a short tree branch in half.

"Lord, you're depressing," Grist said. "If you were a fish, I bet the shadow of a sparrow would make you go belly-up."

The man with the crippled arm did not take kindly to being the butt of their humor. Glaring, he poked at the fire, muttering, "It's better to be safe than sorry, as my pa always said. Just because I tell it like I see it doesn't give you call to step on my toes."

"Sheathe your claws, you nit-brain. I didn't mean anything by it," Grist apologized. Glancing at Jipala, he said, "What's your opinion, 'breed? You haven't said six words all day. Sometimes you're worse than your friend Cuchillo."

Jipala grunted. "I think that all white men talk too much. Listening to you is like listening to chipmunks chatter."

Meanwhile, Flavius was crawling closer and closer. He was within a stone's throw of the women when he glanced at the men again to see how Cuchillo had taken Grist's remark. To his utter consternation, he realized that Cuchillo was not present and had been absent the whole time.

But if not there, where was he?

Behind Flavius the grass rustled. He whirled, or tried to, but this time Little Hickory was not on hand to come to his rescue. His head exploded with pain. The stars danced crazily. And the earth rushed up to meet his face.

Chapter Ten

Few things will snap a man out of fatigue faster than having the business end of a cocked rifle shoved into his face.

Davy Crockett stiffened, raising his arms to show that he was not inclined to resist. His befuddled head clearing, he bestowed his most amiable smile on the scruffy quartet. "What's wrong, gents? There's plenty of room for you to swing that canoe on around. This river is wide enough for all of us."

"Friendly cuss, ain't he?" stated the man in the stern.

"But he doesn't listen worth spit," responded the big man holding the rifle. Eyes narrowing, he said to Davy, "I won't tell you twice to get down, mister."

Maybe it was the lack of sleep. Maybe it was the fact that Davy had an instinctive dislike for anyone who pointed a gun at him. Or maybe he was just plain feeling ornery. Whatever the reason, he roosted where he was and replied, "If I had the time, I'd teach you some manners, friend. But as it is, a Dakota war party is dogging my heels and I don't have the time to waste."

The mention of the Sioux alarmed the four. Each brandished a pistol or a rifle and peered past Davy up the Missouri. "The Dakotas, you say?" declared the big man. "Damn it all! Just our luck!"

A beanpole whose bushy brows nearly hid his eyes gave Davy a stern look. "It wasn't very smart of you to get the Sioux riled, stranger. What did you do to them?"

Davy did not feel very kindly disposed toward these men. They were gruff and arrogant and treated him poorly. But they were fellow whites, and if the Sioux caught them, they would be slain even though they were not the ones the Sioux were after. Which they plainly weren't. The Oglala had mentioned that four women had been stolen, and these men did not have any women with them.

"It's not me the Dakotas mainly want," Davy answered. "I just happened to be in the wrong place at the wrong time." He nudged the sorrel to the right of the canoe, and no one tried to stop him. "They have three war parties out hunting for a pack of no-account white jackals who stole some women from their kinsmen, the Oglalas, three or four days ago."

Utter amazement etched the faces of the quartet. "You don't say!" exclaimed their big leader.

The beanpole lowered his flintlock. "How is it that the Oglalas think whites are to blame? And how did the Dakotas hear about it so soon? I mean, the Oglalas live a far piece south of here."

"The Oglalas sent a rider who rode his horse into the ground," Davy explained. "As for your first question, I understand the Oglalas found tracks of white men in some mud along the Missouri. That gave them the clue."

"Mighty careless of those whites," said the big man, who for some reason shifted to scowl at the heaviest of the others. "Wouldn't you say, Clem?"

Before Clem could respond, the beanpole smiled at Davy, exposing two blackened front teeth. "My name is Gallows. My friends and me are on our way to the Rockies to join a company of trappers. It's a blessin' that we ran into you, mister, or we'd've had our hair skinned off. We're in your debt."

"Yep," chimed in the big man. "What say we hook up and head on back down the river together? Five guns are better than four." He paused, then held out a hand the size of a bear's paw. "I'm Garth Shaw, by the way."

Davy shook. The man had a grip like a steel trap.

"Sorry about shoving my gun at you the way I done," Shaw said. "But not all white men you meet out here are friendly. Some are killers and thieves and worse. I was just being careful."

"No harm done," Davy said. The invitation to join up with them appealed to him. As Shaw had noted, there *was* strength in numbers. If the Sioux caught up, he'd need all the help he could get. "I like your idea. I'll stick to the shore and you can stay out in the middle. That way, whether the Sioux come at us from either side or from the rear, one of us is bound to spot them."

"Sounds good to me," Shaw agreed. As one of the others raised a paddle, he said, "How far off do you reckon the Dakotas are, by the way?"

"There's no telling," Davy said, and clucked the sorrel to the west shore. He had been wondering the same thing himself. Depending on how soon the Tetons had discovered he was missing and lit out after him, he had anywhere from a three- to five-hour lead. Probably less, since Struck-By-Blackfeet would be thirsting for his blood.

The canoe swung about to head downriver. Shaw and Gallows took over the paddling, and they were quite skilled. Davy had to hold his mount to a canter to keep up.

As yet there had been no sign of Flavius. Davy prayed that his friend was still alive, and that Flavius had the good sense to make for the river after they were separated. It was the only water to be had for miles around, and it provided the only decent cover.

Davy doubted that his friend would have left for home. Not without him. Back in Tennessee there were folks who did not rate Flavius as the best of companions. Too loud, they would say. Too timid, others might add. But Flavius had never given Davy cause to complain. The man would do to ride the hills with anytime.

But was Flavius alive? That was the crucial question. Davy had his fingers crossed, yet it bothered him that none of the Sioux hunting party had seen his friend. Either Flavius had lain low and avoided them, or by sheer luck the Dakotas had not crossed his path.

The morning dragged by. Davy's fatigue returned to plague him. Rest would have to wait, though, until he was absolutely convinced he had given the Tetons the slip.

By noon the sorrel was in need of a break. Davy waved to the trappers, then reined up. As he was loosening the cinch, the canoe coasted to within a few feet of the bank.

"What's wrong, friend?" Shaw inquired. "Has your horse gone lame?"

"It needs a breather," Davy explained.

Gallows gazed up the Missouri. "Is that wise, what with the country swarmin' with heathens and all? A fellow never knows when those red devils will pop up. You'd be better off resting at the end of the day."

Davy nodded at the sweaty lather on the animal's chest. "I've been riding all night. If I don't stop here and now, this horse is liable to play out on me. Then I'd be even worse off."

"Suit yourself," Shaw said. "But we have friends camped down the river a piece. They got to be warned. If we push, we can reach them by sunset."

"Go on, then," Davy coaxed.

Shaw dipped his paddle in and stroked backward to turn the canoe. "We'll stay at their camp until morning. Catch up with us by then and you're welcome to join our outfit for protection."

"Thanks for the offer."

Gallows waved. "Watch your hair, friend. I'd hate to see you lose that fine rifle to a filthy Injun. I wouldn't mind owning that my own self."

"That's right," interjected Clem, the stocky one. "You take real good care of what fixins you've got." Strangely, he chuckled, and was slapped on the shoulder by Gallows.

In seconds the canoe was cleaving the water like an otter. It swept around the next bend, none of the trappers giving a backward glance.

Davy had mixed feelings about seeing them go. Their guns would have helped keep the Sioux at bay, but there was something about the quartet that made him uneasy, something he could not quite put his finger on.

Shrugging off his uneasy thoughts as a result of not enough sleep, Davy allowed the sorrel to drink. While it did, he hiked his buckskin shirt to splash water on his chest, neck, and face. His stomach growled. He was sorry that he had not thought to ask the trappers if they had a scrap of food they could do without. As it was, he would not get to eat until evening.

Fifteen minutes was all Davy could spare. Then he was back in the saddle. For a while it felt so nice to be riding along with the wind in his hair and the sun on his face that he forgot about the Dakotas. His reminder came in the form of a high-pitched whinny to the southwest.

Davy immediately stopped. Off through the trees was a knot of riders, rapidly approaching. He did not need a spyglass to see that they were Sioux. It was the band Black Buffalo had sent to scour the country bordering the river to the west.

Had they somehow seen him? Davy angled the sorrel into the densest growth available and, alighting, pinched the sorrel's nostrils to keep it from nickering to the mounts of the Sioux, who presently entered the trees and made straight for the Missouri.

They had come to water their warhorses. Nineteen warriors, all told, armed with a variety of weapons. While their steeds indulged, they huddled to confer.

Davy did not take his hand off the sorrel. He would be safe so long as he kept the animal quiet. It fidgeted, stomping a hoof, so he slapped its leg.

A number of the Tetons walked off into the bushes. Davy saw one man hitch down his pants, and turned away. He was startled to see another warrior riding into the strip of woodland from the plain, a straggler whose horse appeared to have a sore foot. He was even more startled when the Dakota looked directly at his hiding place.

Be calm, Davy told himself. The warrior could

not possibly know he was there. Then, out of the corner of his eye, he registered movement. Twisting, he saw the same thing the warrior had seen: The sorrel's tail was swishing from side to side.

The straggler reined his animal toward them.

It was only a matter of seconds before the warrior spotted the sorrel. If he yelled, every last member of the war party would converge.

Davy coiled, marking the newcomer's progress. The man had a bow in hand and was reaching over his back for an arrow from his quiver. Davy pulled the reins taut. When the Sioux looked down to nock the shaft to the sinew string, Davy vaulted into the saddle, slapped his legs, and exploded from the high growth in a shower of leaves and broken limbs.

At a gallop, Davy deliberately slammed the sorrel into the other man's paint. Both horses staggered, but the smaller paint was not able to keep its footing and crashed into a briar patch, spilling its rider, whose bow became snagged by thorns.

Davy sped around and out to the prairie, then immediately reined to the left and hugged the vegetation. Whoops and shouts signified that the Sioux had spied him and were rushing to their own horses to give chase.

Nothing ever went right! Davy mused wryly. The sorrel was still tired and could not maintain its swift gait for long. The Sioux would hog-tie him right quick unless inspiration struck.

It did. Spawned by desperation, a lunatic idea made Davy rein to the left again, back *into* the trees. Weaving among the trunks, avoiding a long log, he galloped to a short slope, which he descended on the fly. Beyond was a gravel bar, poking a third of the way into the Missouri.

The sorrel executed a flying jump, landing in

waist-high water, drenching Davy from the waist down. To the north the Indians were flying toward the prairie. None realized that he had doubled back on himself. Not yet, anyway.

Flowers covered most of the opposite bank. The sorrel scrambled up, then shook itself. Davy picked the rockiest route into a cluster of oak trees. Ground-hitching the horse, he pulled his legs up onto the saddle so he could straighten and grab a limb. From his vantage point he watched the Sioux milling about near where he had reentered the trees. In under a minute they did likewise, a powerfully built Dakota in the lead, half hanging from his warhorse in order to better read the sign.

At the Missouri the warriors disputed angrily. Some were for following the river to the south, some to the north, and others pointed at the far side.

Finally they split up. The majority rushed to the right and left, leaving three men to ford the river. Strung out in a row, lances and bows at the ready, they scoured the growth, which was thicker on the east side of the Missouri than on the west.

Davy dropped from the limb onto the sorrel and lit out. It would not take the trio long to find his trail. But he had another trick up his sleeve that might just lose them.

Truth to tell, it was the same trick he had just used. Riding in a wide loop to the south, he plunged into the river again, this time bearing to the south instead of crossing.

The way he had it figured, he was safer there than anywhere else. The warriors who had gone north would never spot him, and the ten or so Sioux who had already gone south were far enough ahead that it was unlikely he would stumble onto them.

That left the three who had crossed the Missouri. By sticking to the water, he ensured they would not find his trail again.

For a while all went well. Davy saw neither hide nor hair of any of the Dakotas. He was closer to the west side than the east, passing under a tree that grew at the river's edge. Shadows flitted across him as branches overhead blotted out the brilliant sunlight.

Davy did not think anything of it when one of the shadows seemed to move. Then he saw a horse by itself up on the bank. It was the paint he had rammed into a short while ago, the one belonging to the straggler. And if the horse was there, its owner had to be nearby.

A five-ton boulder seemed to slam into Davy's shoulders, smashing him from the saddle. The breath whooshed from his lungs at the brutal impact. He crashed to earth with his legs in the water, his chest on dry land.

Davy wrenched to the right as a glittering knife thudded into the soil an inch from his ear. Astride his stomach was the warrior who owned the paint. Nicks and scrapes dotted the warrior's torso and limbs where the thorns had bit into his flesh.

The Dakota hissed a few words in his own language. Davy did not comprehend, but their meaning was not hard to guess. It was probably something along the lines of "Now I'm going to cut out your heart, you white bastard!"

Again the knife flashed, sticking into the ground under Davy's left arm. Davy landed a right cross to the jaw that swayed the Teton but was not strong enough to knock him out.

Unfazed but wary, the warrior jumped erect and

began to work around behind Davy. An old hand at blade fighting, Davy knew just what the wily warrior was up to. He swiftly backpedaled, evading slashes that would have opened him like a gutted fish, until he bumped into a tree.

The warrior seized the moment. Growling, he stabbed high, a feint for his true thrust, which speared low.

Davy came within a hair's width of never siring more children. The knife thudded into the tree below his crotch. It wedged fast, forcing the Sioux to tug on the hilt. Not about to let the man free it, Davy slugged him twice in lightning succession, rocking the Teton on his heels.

Somewhere down the river, someone was shouting.

The Sioux, having lost his grip on the knife, sprang to meet Davy as Davy slid in close to land another punch. The warrior sidestepped, then pounced, his iron fingers wrapping around Davy's neck, his thumbs clawing into Davy's throat. A knee caught Davy in the groin and they both went down, Davy on the bottom again.

Victory shone in the warrior's eyes. His shoulders were wide, packed with muscle, and he exerted every sinew in an effort to throttle Davy.

Air no longer reached Davy's lungs. He tried to inhale again and again but could not catch a breath. Gripping the Sioux's hands, he attempted to pry them off, but it was if they had been glued to his skin. He heaved. He pushed. There was no dislodging his foe.

Davy rammed a knee into the Teton's stomach. Once. Twice. Three times. In each instance the man stiffened and grimaced but gamely continued to strangle Davy. A fourth blow, a heel to the kidney, accomplished what the others had not. Crying out, the man jerked a hand behind him.

It was the opening Davy needed. His right fist caught the Dakota under the jaw, partially lifting the warrior off him. His left folded the man's stomach. A flip to the side, and Davy scrambled into a crouch.

The yelling downriver had grown louder. Whoever it was drew closer by the second.

Starting to rise, the Dakota threw his head high and roared an answer.

Help would be on the way, Davy knew. He had moments to prevail or all would be lost.

In the swirl of combat they had moved from the river's edge into the woods. Behind the Teton, and perhaps unknown to him, was a log. It was not very long or very high, but it was just what Davy needed.

Suddenly charging, fists windmilling, Davy drove the warrior back. The man was so intent on avoiding the punches that he tripped over the log. With a leap, Davy was on the Dakota before he could rise. A solid jab followed by a left cross left the warrior sprawled senseless on the grass.

Winded, Davy found his rifle, then ran to the sorrel, which had climbed out of the water. The warrior doing the yelling was so close that Davy could hear the twigs crunch.

Taking the sorrel by the reins, Davy dashed to the paint, which nickered but did not run off. Davy remedied that by smacking the stock of his rifle against its flank. It obliged by crashing westward through the brush while whinnying shrilly.

Quickly, Davy steered the sorrel into a thicket. None too soon. A pair of Sioux rushed around the next bend, caught a glimpse, if that, of the fleeing paint, and galloped off after it, never noticing their unconscious companion.

"The luck of the Irish," Davy said under his breath. Mounting, he hesitated. The shouts were bound to bring warriors from all directions. Since there were fewer to the east, that was the place to be.

Consequently, Davy forded the Missouri River one more time. He took shelter in a ravine that linked the bottomland to a ridge. On a narrow shelf screened by boulders and some pines, he slid off and found a spot where he enjoyed an unobstructed view of not only the river below but the vast grassland beyond.

True to his prediction, the Sioux were gathering from all points of the compass. The trio who had crossed a while ago were now recrossing. One of them must have found the warrior Davy had felled. His whoop guided the rest.

At the same time, the pair who had gone after the paint caught it a few hundred yards away.

Davy closely observed the palaver that ensued. After considerable jawing and gesturing, the band divided itself in half. Some went north, the rest out on the prairie. He nodded, pleased. Their line of reasoning was not hard to savvy. Since the warriors rushing to the south, north, and east had not spied him, they logically concluded he had gone west. Just as he counted on.

Staying put until the last of them were out of sight, Davy forked leather and resumed his trek. He had been delayed so long that it was unlikely he would find the trappers' camp before nightfall, but he tried his best.

The sun had been gone over an hour when an acrid whiff of smoke tingled Davy's nose. Until that moment he had been plodding along the shoreline with his head on his chest, so tired that a child with a feather could have swatted him off.

Snapping awake, he searched for the fire that had to be close by. A gust of wind helped. Fingers of flame several hundred feet ahead flared brighter, serving as a beacon.

Soon Davy distinguished a clearing and people—trappers, evidently—clustered near the center. Making no attempt to sneak up on them for fear one of the trappers would mistake him for an Indian and open fire, he rode close enough for them to hear him shout, "Hello, the camp! Garth Shaw, are you there?"

A flurry of activity greeted the hail. Moments later Shaw's gravel voice responded. "Stranger, is that you? The one in the coonskin cap? You never did tell us your name."

"Crockett," Davy said. As he reached the clearing, men materialized on all sides, nine in all, two whose visages hinted at Indian blood. Past them, blanketed by shadows, were other people Davy could not quite make out, people who appeared to be asleep.

"Glad to see you made it, friend," Gallows said, his gaze lingering more on Davy's rifle than on Davy.

"Any sign of the Dakotas?" asked Shaw.

Davy gave them an abbreviated version of his clash, ending with "They'll be along soon enough. My best guess would be about noon tomorrow."

A man almost as big as Shaw grinned and said, "Let 'em. We'll be long gone by then. They'll never catch our canoes."

The aroma of perking coffee made Davy's mouth water. "Mind sharing some of that brew?"

"Not at all," Shaw said. "Hop on down and help yourself. There's stew left over if you're hungry."

The trappers moved back to make room for Davy to dismount. He was so tired that only then did he realize they had the sorrel surrounded. "I'm grateful," he declared, but he hesitated, disturbed by a feeling that something was not quite as it should be.

Over in the shadows someone snorted, then grunted three times and sat up.

"Looks as if our other guest has come around at last," Gallows remarked. Most of the trappers chortled.

"Who are you talking about?" Davy asked, sliding his right foot from its stirrup.

The man in the shadows was the one who replied. "Davy? Is that you I hear? My God, light a rag elsewhere! These men are slavers, Davy! Slavers!"

Chapter Eleven

A split second before Flavius Harris hollered, Davy Crockett saw two of the shadowy figures near him sit up. Bathed by the feeble glow of the fire, their silhouettes revealed both to be females. In that instant Davy realized who Shaw and the others must be. They weren't trappers at all. They were the culprits sought by the Dakotas, the whites who made their living by stealing Indian women. The yell of his friend just confirmed it.

That split-second edge saved Davy's life. For when Flavius yelled, Shaw and company closed in, some reaching for the sorrel's bridle, some bringing their weapons to bear, others lunging at Davy. But Davy's rifle was pointing at the ground at Shaw's feet at that crucial moment. A snap of his wrist, a flick of the thumb, and Davy had the muzzle trained on Shaw's sternum, the hammer cocked. "No one move!" he directed. "Or else!"

To a man, the slavers turned to statues in their

tracks. Shaw stared at Liz, blanching. "You heard him!" he roared. "Anyone who doesn't listen will answer to me!"

Gallows and a half-breed were nearest to Davy. They obeyed, but they were not pleased. Gallows, in particular, fidgeted eagerly, anxious to grab Davy's leg and topple him from the saddle.

Davy bent toward Shaw. "Have them back off five steps and lower their weapons," he commanded. "One wrong move on their part, and come tomorrow the buzzards will be feasting on your carcass."

Hatred contorted the big cutthroat's features. "Pull that trigger and you lose your edge. My boys will be on top of you like wolves on a cornered buck."

"That they will," Davy allowed, "but you won't be alive to see it."

Shaw stared at Davy's trigger finger, then snapped, "Do as the Southerner says, boys. He's got us by the short hairs for the moment."

The slavers were a sullen bunch as they paced backward the required number of steps and set their various guns and knives at their feet.

"Now have them take another five steps back and reach for the stars," Davy said. To emphasize his request, he gouged the muzzle against the tip of Shaw's nose.

"Do it!"

Over in the shadows, Flavius was practically beside himself with glee. So what if he was hog-tied? So what if his head felt as if a drummer in a marching band had been practicing on it? So what if he was far from out of danger? Davy was there! He was reunited with his friend! Come what may, they would face it together.

Davy started to knee the sorrel to the right to

put Shaw between himself and the slavers.

"Think you're smart, don't you, mister?" the big man said. "But you've just cut your own throat. With the Dakotas on the warpath, you and your friend over there won't last two days." Shaw nodded at Flavius. "You would have been better off hooking up with our outfit."

"Am I wearing diapers?" Davy countered. "Who do you think you're fooling? You never meant to have me tag along. I'd have been dead the second my feet touched the ground."

That Shaw did not dispute it proved to Davy his guess was right. Holding Liz steady, he slid to the ground, then motioned for Shaw to precede him over to where his partner waited. All four women had sat up and scooted forward on their knees to better observe the proceedings.

"It's lucky for you that you have horses and we don't," Shaw said. "Otherwise, we'd ride you down and stake you on an anthill."

Davy had not noticed it before, but Flavius's dun was tied to a tree that bordered the clearing. They could light a shuck and the slavers would never catch them. Except for one tiny hitch: the four women.

Flavius showed all his teeth and declared, "Brother, are you a sight for sore eyes! I'd about given up hope of ever seeing you again. What happened? Where have you been?"

"Another time," Davy said, halting Shaw by jabbing him in the back. Circling, he drew his butcher knife, hunkered, and carefully sliced the rope that bound his friend's wrists. He gave the knife to Flavius, who excitedly removed the ankle rope.

"Now let's cross the Missouri and head east! If a local tribe is out for white blood, I'd rather be long gone when they get here."

141

David Thompson

"We can't," Davy said.

Flavius, rubbing his sore wrists, looked up. He knew that tone. Oh God, how he knew that tone! It always spelled trouble with a capital *T*. "What do you mean?" he asked, then saw that Davy was gazing at the four captives. "Oh, no!" he bleated. "Tell me that you're not thinking what I think you're thinking."

"We have to take them to their people."

An arrogant, brittle laugh rumbled from Shaw. "Go right ahead, Good Samaritan. I'd love to be there when the Oglalas carve you into little pieces."

"*I* wouldn't!" Flavius exclaimed. Rising unsteadily, his legs tingling, he helped himself to one of the discarded rifles and covered the slavers. "Davy, you can't be serious. Let's just untie them and let them run off on their own. I'm sure they can find their way home again by themselves."

"What if they run into an enemy raiding party? Or into a grizzly or some such?" Shaking his head, Davy stepped several yards to the right so Shaw could not jump him and tucked the stock of his rifle in the crook of his right elbow to free his hands for making sign talk. In essence, he told the women, "Do not be afraid. My friend and I are your friends. We will cut you loose and help you make it back to your village."

The women exchanged astounded expressions.

"Free them," Davy instructed his friend.

Agitated enough to spit nails, Flavius complied. It never failed. Just when he thought that things were finally going in their favor, Davy had to go and put them in even greater peril. He made himself a promise. *If* they lived through this nightmare, and *if* they somehow made it safely back to Tennessee, and *if* Davy ever had the gall to come over and ask him to go on another gallivant, he was going to punch Davy right in the nose.

One of the women appeared to be slightly older than the rest, and it was she who, after rubbing her wrists and forearms for over a minute, signed to Davy, "I am Eagle Woman, an Oglala. Why would you, a white man like these other whites, want to help us, who are your enemies?"

"Just as not all Dakotas are alike, neither are all whites," Davy tactfully signed. "These other white men are as much my enemies as they are yours." He paused. "As for helping you, a Sioux couple recently helped me. It is only fair that I repay the favor."

A younger woman, more timid than the rest, fearfully regarded their captors and signed, "How will we get away from these bad men? On foot? Or do you have more horses hidden nearby?"

"I wish I did," Davy signed. He had been debating how best to effect their escape and saw only one means. It entailed a great sacrifice on his part and Flavius's, but the lives of the four women made it worthwhile. "We will take the canoes that you were brought in."

Flavius, confused by the strange hand gestures his friend was making, and desperate to understand what was going on, saw the four women glance toward the canoes. "Terrific idea! They take the canoes and we take our horses! All's well that ends well!"

"We're all leaving in canoes," Davy told him.

"You and me too?" Flavius said. His fleeting hope that everything would turn out just fine had been dashed. "What about our horses? Once we're shed of the females, we'll be stranded afoot."

"We can paddle harder and faster than they can," Davy said. "Plus they'll need us to protect them if they run into trouble before we reach their country."

"But the *horses!*" Flavius protested, stunned by the implication. "Why, I've had that dun since Hector was a pup. Contrary as the critter is, it rides like a rocking chair sits. I won't just run off and leave it! I won't!"

Davy knew it was best to pay Flavius no mind when his friend was in a funk. Motioning at the women, he signed, "Pick two canoes for our use. Push the others out into the river so the current will carry them away."

"We will do as you want," Eagle Woman signed. They rushed off to obey.

Flavius's misgivings were mounting by the moment. "Let's talk this over, hoss," he cautioned. "Think of how hard it will be for us to reach Tennessee without mounts. It'll take us a month of Sundays alone just to get to Westport Landing." The trading post was the farthest outpost of civilization, located where the Missouri and Kansas rivers met.

"Fetch the dun," Davy directed, swinging toward the slavers. So far Shaw and the rest were behaving themselves, but he had no illusions about what would occur if he let down his guard.

The leader glowered like a bear at bay. "Without our canoes the Tetons are bound to find us. What you're fixing to do is the same as cold-blooded murder."

"It's no worse than what you aimed to do to me," Davy responded. "No different than what I suspect you've done to a heap of others over the years."

"You'd best kill us, then," Shaw said flatly. "Because I promise you here and now that if you don't, I'll hunt you down if it takes the rest of my life."

"Provided you live out the week." Davy could not resist rubbing it in.

The other slavers were listening intently. "Shaw, we can't let them go off in our canoes," Gallows called out. "It's suicide if we do."

"Yeah," interjected a man with a withered arm whose name Davy did not know. "We should rush him. He's only one man, and there are nine of us."

"It's better that he drops one or two rather than have the Dakotas wipe us all out," opined a stocky cutthroat.

Over a shoulder Shaw said, "Stay where you are, damn it! We're not beaten yet. The Apaches couldn't lick us. The Mexican army couldn't lick us. And no damn hick from the South is going to lick us, either."

Davy smiled. "But I'll sure try." To Flavius, who was pouting, he said, "Find your possibles if you know where they are. Your rifle and pistols are on the ground yonder."

Too depressed for words, Flavius mechanically trudged over and reclaimed his own weapons. Any other time, that would have been cause for celebration. Now he only wanted to dig a hole, crawl in, and pull the dirt back down on top of him. He had an awful feeling that Davy was going to get them slaughtered. After gathering an armful of the slavers' guns, Flavius walked to the shore, waded a few feet into the shallows, and let go. Water seeped into his moccasins, soaking his feet, but he did not care. He was a doomed man anyway, so what did a little discomfort matter?

"No!" Grist bellowed, taking a few strides.

"You son of a bitch!" added Kline, doing the same.

Davy swung Liz to cover them. "Not another step!" he warned. They stopped, quivering with suppressed fury. It would not take much to incite them or the others into a rash attack.

The women had shoved one of the canoes out into the Missouri and were applying their backs to the second. Gliding smoothly through the tranquil water, it was enveloped by the night.

Gallows spun toward their leader. "Damn it, Shaw! Don't just stand there like a bump on a log. *Do something!* We're doomed if we don't."

"Stay calm," Shaw advised. "Our time will come."

Davy decided to speed things along. "Turn around," he ordered, and when Shaw begrudgingly pivoted, he gripped the bigger man by the back of the shirt, shoving him toward the dun. "Untie it."

Flavius was too distraught to protest. He stood meekly as his friend whooped and waved an arm to spook his mount into trotting off into the brush. There went his sole chance to ever cuddle with Matilda again.

Davy had Shaw spook the sorrel. It pained him to abandon a horse that had served him in such excellent stead for so many arduous months. His sole consolation was that the pair would not want for forage, not with the well-nigh limitless grassland at their disposal. In time, perhaps roving Indians would find them. The sorrel would make a fine warhorse.

Flavius was carrying the last of the rifles to the Missouri. One must belong to Cuchillo, the 'breed who had knocked him senseless, because Cuchillo glared when he held it out. Smirking, Flavius slowly lowered it into the water.

Eagle Woman and her Oglala sisters had pushed the last two canoes into the shallows and climbed in. Beckoning, she signed urgently to Davy,

"Hurry. The bad men have the look of rattlesnakes about to strike."

That they did. Davy retreated to Flavius's side. Together they stepped to the canoes. "You shove off first. I'll be right behind you."

Two smooth-faced maidens looked expectantly at Flavius as he eased over the side. They were scared and it showed. After the horrors they had been through, who could blame them? Grudgingly, Flavius realized that Davy was right; it was their duty to escort the maidens home.

"Don't fret, ladies," Flavius said quietly. "My friend and me will have you back in your own lodges in three shakes of a lamb's tail."

One handed him a short paddle. Flavius experimented to find a grip he liked, then commenced to stroke in a steady if awkward cadence. His experience with canoes was almost as limited as his experience with the fairer sex, but he did not want the women to brand him a simpleton, so he forged gamely on, poised on his knees in the bow, slanting toward the middle of the river.

In his haste to get away, Flavius had overlooked the trivial detail that he could not swim any better than a rock. Suddenly, with dark, swirling water on both sides of him, the old fear coursed through him like a red-hot poker. He recollected how he had nearly drowned not too long ago, recalling how it felt to have his air choked off and his lungs at the point of total collapse.

On the shore, Davy gave his friend a thirty-second lead before he slid into a canoe with Eagle Woman and another Oglala who was not much older than eighteen winters, if that.

None of the slavers had moved. Gallows was gnashing his teeth like a rabid wolverine, while two half-breeds were stooped forward like runners about to begin a race.

"Be seeing you," Davy called out to Shaw, who did not elect to answer. Swiftly setting Liz down, he scooped up a paddle and dipped it into the Missouri. Stroking furiously, he backed away from the shoreline.

The moment the rifle was no longer in his hands, the slavers exploded into action. Both 'breeds dashed to where Flavius had dumped their guns and dived in. Gallows and others were right behind, goading them on.

Shaw snaked a hand behind his back. When it reappeared, he held a single-shot derringer. Rushing to the river, he paralleled it, striving for a clear shot.

Davy was twenty feet out and widening that gap by the second. Cloaked in darkness, he hunched forward and motioned for Eagle Woman and the other Oglala to imitate him. Seconds later the derringer cracked. The lead ball missed the canoe, striking the surface near the stern and spraying water onto the young maiden.

Paddling rapidly, Davy guided the canoe on down the Missouri. The last sight he had of the slavers was of Shaw cursing a blue streak while the 'breeds tossed soaked guns to their fellows on the shore. Gallows was shaking a fist at the Missouri and railing fiercely.

When the canoe swept past the first bend, Davy bestowed a smile on the former captives. "We have done it," he signed. "You are safe now."

"I thank you for what you have done," Eagle Woman replied, "but we will never be safe until we are with our own kind once again."

Davy kept his eyes skinned for his friend. He need not have bothered. For out of the gloom came Flavius's voice, laden with anxiety.

"Davy? Is that you back there?"

"It's me," Davy verified.

Flavius exhaled the breath he had not realized he was holding. The shot had scared him into thinking he might need to escort the women home by his lonesome. "Care to swing around in front of me so you can lead?" he hollered.

"You can handle it."

"I'm not so sure," Flavius was inclined to say, but he held his tongue. Starlight was all he had to navigate by, barely enough for him to see the fingers at the end of his arm. The darkness clung to him like a living creature, the gloom deepening the farther they traveled.

The shorelines did not help much, buried as they were in blackness reminiscent of the Pit. Thick trees and high brush formed a jumbled black shape that framed the waterway from end to end.

Flavius was worried that he would drift too close to land and strike a snag, or else pile onto one of the many small islands that dotted the Missouri. Either would damage the canoe, maybe severely. Whenever an object loomed in front of him, he swerved aside. Once he had to strike a small log with the paddle to prevent a collision.

Sweat broke out across Flavius's forehead. There was no telling what sort of obstacles they might encounter. In his humble opinion, his partner had been addlepated to risk the river at night.

Forty feet to the north, Davy Crockett swelled his chest, invigorated by the brisk breeze. The splash of Flavius's paddle guided him.

Davy was glad to be free of the slavers. He relaxed for the first time since fleeing from the Tetons. Hunger gnawed at his vitals, but it also kept his fatigue at bay.

149

The women did not make a peep. They knelt with their hands primly in their laps, surveying the countryside with wide eyes, as if the night harbored demons worse than those they had just fled. It led Davy to wonder if they had ever been abroad at night before they were abducted.

Many Indians, like whites, seldom ventured far from their dwellings once the sun went down. Davy never had understood why. To him, the wilderness was the same at night as it was during the day except for the absence of the sun. But some grown men of his acquaintance would not venture out in the dark for all the gold in Midas's treasury.

Flavius was one. It tickled Davy's funny bone that his friend, who had tangled with black bears and wolves and hostile Indians, was as scared of the dark as a kid of nine.

A squeal up ahead was followed by a rending crash. Davy slowed, hearing a frantic series of splashes and Flavius hollering for someone to hold on. "What's happened?" he shouted, unable to see them yet.

Flavius was embarrassed to say. Thinking that something large had moved on the west bank, he had glanced toward shore. His attention had been diverted for only a fraction of a second, but that had been more than enough time for disaster to strike. For when he swung forward, he saw the upthrust jagged rim of a submerged boulder or rock outcropping right in front of the canoe.

One of the Oglalas had seen it, too. She squealed a warning.

The canoe struck the outcropping just past the bow. Wood splintered like so much kindling. The jolt of impact swung the canoe violently to the left and the woman in the center flew over the side.

She managed to grasp the rim as she was going under.

"Hold on!" Flavius bawled, paddling for all he was worth to straighten the canoe so he could head for shore. A clammy sensation on his legs warned him that they might not make it. Water was gushing in through the gap. Already it was an inch deep and rising quickly.

The other Oglala grabbed her friend's arms so she would not slip off.

Flavius pumped his arms from side to side. The stricken canoe swung first to the left, then to the right, then back again. He could not hold a steady course if his life depended on it. Which it did.

Suddenly the canoe was jarred by a bump at the rear. Flavius glanced around, and whooped. "Remind me to treat you to a jug when we get back!"

Davy had caught up with them, perceived their plight, and deliberately but gently rammed his canoe into theirs, adding his momentum to theirs, pushing them that much farther toward the west bank. He matched his paddle strokes to those of Flavius so the two canoes would stay close together.

A gravel bar materialized. Flavius powered the bow up onto it and leaped out while the canoe was still moving. Darting to the woman who was hanging on at the stern, he hauled her to her feet.

"We did it!" Flavius cried as Davy's canoe slid up onto the bar beside his. "We're safe, thanks to you!"

At that juncture a familiar voice rent the night to the north. The leader of the slavers roared, "Hear that? It's them! We've caught up with those bastards already!"

Chapter Twelve

No one was more surprised at Garth Shaw's triumphant cry than Davy Crockett. He saw that the stricken canoe would never float again, so escape down the river was no longer feasible. Springing out, he signed to Eagle Woman, "Take your friends into the trees, quickly. We must hide."

As one, the women surged erect and raced across the gravel bar, the Oglala who had been dunked being assisted by two of her friends.

Flavius thought that he saw something out on the water, moving in their direction. He raised his rifle to shoot, but Davy pushed the barrel.

"Save your lead for when they get in close. That's when we'll need it most."

"It just ain't possible that they've found us so fast," Flavius said, falling into step beside his friend. "Where did we go wrong?"

Any answer Davy might have given was forestalled by another yell to the north. Only this one came from the shore, not the river. "We heard them too, Garth! Move in and we'll box them between us!"

That was Gallows, Davy guessed. He saw the Oglalas come to a steep bank and begin to scramble up it. Joining them, he gave Eagle Woman a boost, then tensed at the thud of hooves and the crash of brush to their right.

"Oh, God!" Flavius exclaimed. "They caught our horses, too? What else can possibly go wrong?"

As if in answer, a narrow strip of bank inexplicably collapsed, spilling two of the women in a cascade of dirt. Davy and Flavius each helped one to stand.

"Hurry to the top!" Davy signed, the drumming growing nearer and nearer. As he gave the maiden a push, a gun cracked. The ball whined off a rock close to Flavius, who tore up the bank as if his britches were on fire.

Davy whirled, bringing up Liz. A shadowy form emerged out of the darkness, bearing down on them at a breakneck gallop. It was hard for Davy to distinguish between the rider and the horse, so he delayed squeezing the trigger an extra few seconds. Steel glinted dully as the slaver drew a knife or tomahawk.

Hoping that it was Gallows, Davy stroked the trigger. Liz boomed, spewing smoke. The man flung his arms heavenward as if in supplication for his soul, then pitched to the left and toppled, rolling the final few yards to stop almost at Davy's feet.

The man had been astride the dun. Davy grabbed for it, but the horse swerved and kept on going.

Flavius gained the top, then turned to cover his friend. Mentally cursing his stupid horse, he

153

glanced at the base of the bank and recognized the dead man. "That was Weist," he whispered as Davy bounded up the slope like a lithe panther.

"One down, only eight to go."

"*Only* eight?" Flavius said, not at all heartened by the odds.

From out on the Missouri rose Garth Shaw's voice again. "Gallows? Weist? Did you get one of those stinking Tennesseans?"

Davy cupped a hand to his mouth to reply. "It's the other way around, vermin! Come close enough and we'll do the same to you and all your boys!"

The night grew as quiet as a graveyard. Davy cocked his head and detected the swish of paddles being stealthily used. Nudging his companion, he jogged after the women, who had reached the vegetation and paused to wait for Flavius and him.

"Give us knives and we will fight," Eagle Woman signed.

Davy appreciated her offer, and he had no doubt they could hold their own. As he had learned from the couple who befriended him, Teton women, like their men, rated courage as a supreme virtue. They would fight to the death, if need be, in defense of their villages and their families.

"I would like to," Davy signed, "but my friend and I will need them. Take cover until this fight is over. If the bad men beat us, you must head north. A party of Tetons is coming to rescue you."

Eagle Woman did a tender thing. She lightly touched his chin, then took charge of her younger sisters and melted into the undergrowth.

Flavius, upset that they were wasting time exchanging silly hand gestures while the slavers closed in, groused, "I wish you would tell me what all that finger flapping is about."

Davy did not respond. A gust of wind had

brought him the thump of a hoof on soft soil. One of the other cutthroats was out there somewhere, mounted on the sorrel.

A scraping noise issued from the vicinity of the gravel bar. Then another. A flurry of whispers preceded a flurry of secretive movement.

"They're fanning out," Flavius whispered.

That they were, Davy realized. Ducking into a thicket, he crouched and placed a hand on his powder horn to commence reloading. He changed his mind when a weaving black figure appeared.

Flavius saw the man too. Elevating his rifle, he steadied it, held his breath, and cocked the hammer.

At the metallic click, the figure promptly vanished as if it had never been there.

Davy nudged his friend, then backed through the thicket until they could straighten. He was about to suggest that they go farther north and try to outflank the killers when a strident screech sent him flying due south instead.

"The women are in trouble," Flavius huffed, struggling to keep up with the fleeter Irishman. Zigzagging through the brush, he relied on Davy's keener eyes to spot obstacles before he did, mimicking every move Davy made. They barreled through high weeds, and Flavius beheld the four women locked in combat with a swarthy cutthroat.

It was one of the 'breeds, Jipala. The man had the youngest maiden by the wrist and was trying to haul her off, but the other three would not let him. He swatted at them with his rifle, holding them at bay, while the youngest woman dug in her heels, resisting mightily.

At the sight of Davy and Flavius, Jipala pivoted.

Snarling like a beast, he threw his captive at her three sisters and was gone, scarcely ruffling the leaves and stems around him.

Flavius had flung his rifle up, but he never got off a shot. Worried that the other half-breed was nearby, and recollecting all too vividly how Cuchillo had sneaked up on him like a ghostly specter, he rotated every which way, trying to watch every approach at once.

Davy gave Eagle Woman and another woman a hand up. None of them had been seriously hurt, although the young one had a bloody gash on her wrist where the slaver's fingernails had broken the skin. Time to change tactics, he mused. Trying to draw their enemies off had not worked.

"We will stay together," Davy signed, and whispered the same aloud for Flavius's benefit, adding, "We've got to find a spot we can defend or we're goners."

"Tell me something I don't know, why don't you?" Flavius jested, but neither of them so much as cracked a grin.

Pointing to the southwest, Davy hurried the women off and brought up the rear to protect them. He had the uneasy feeling that they were being silently shadowed on both sides, yet try as he might, he was not able to spot anyone.

The willows and cottonwoods thickened. Davy could find no place to make a stand. To the east the brush occasionally crackled, reminders that Shaw and his men were still hunting for them.

Eagle Woman came to what appeared to be the lip of a low knoll. She motioned for the other three Oglalas to go around and set an example by swinging to the left.

Davy brought them to a stop by lightly clapping his hands. The knoll was not a knoll at all, but rather a roughly circular hole approximately ten feet in diameter that had been created when a gigantic tree came crashing to earth many years ago. Broken sections of rotting trunk and dead, shattered limbs lay to the west.

"This is it," Davy whispered to Flavius as he dropped to the bottom. The hole was about four feet deep, more than deep enough to conceal them.

The women did not need to be told what to do. In single file they climbed down and huddled in the center.

Flavius had his doubts about stopping, but he hopped in anyway. Hunkering, he ran a hand over the smooth butts of his flintlocks. Of them all, he was the best armed, the one with weapons to spare. He snatched a pistol from under his belt and offered it to Eagle Woman. "Here," he whispered. "In case they get past Davy and me."

The Oglala's eyebrows knitted. She accepted the weapon, then glanced quizzically at both of them.

"I doubt she's ever used one," Davy whispered. Using sign, he briefly explained how to cock the hammer and pull the trigger. Eagle Woman smiled, the first time he had seen her do so, and clasped the pistol to her bosom as if it were manna sent by the Creator.

Something rustled to the northwest. Davy pressed against the earth wall and began reloading, praying there would be no attack until he was ready.

The infernal suspense grated on Flavius's nerves. He tried to tell himself that maybe the slavers would not find their hiding place, that maybe Shaw's outfit would give up and go away. But he was only fooling himself. Jipala and Cuchillo would find them if no one else did. Those two were the most dangerous of the bunch.

Davy had to pour the black powder into Liz's muzzle by touch alone. He had done it so many times that he was able to measure the right amount by the feel of the grains in his palm. Taking a ball from his ammo pouch, he wrapped it in a cloth patch, removed the ramrod, and tamped both down the barrel until they were snugly seated.

Minutes ticked by. Flavius had not heard anything for so long that he entertained the notion Jipala and Cuchillo were not the hellcats he had assumed. The crunch of footsteps and the crackle of limbs from several directions set him straight.

Davy turned toward the forest. The cutthroats were making so much noise that they had to be doing it on purpose. Sure enough, presently a harsh laugh was flung at the hole by Garth Shaw.

"Did you really think you could hide from us, Tennesseean? My 'breeds were shadowing you the whole time, and they fetched us."

Since there was nothing to be gained by not responding, Davy called out, "Do your 'breeds intend to die for you, too? Because that's what they'll do if you rush us."

Garth laughed louder. "Mighty brave talk for a coon who has a fat fool and four worthless squaws to back his play."

Flavius's temper flared at the insult. "Who are you calling a fool, you miserable trash? Step out in the open. We'll settle this man to man."

"Now I'm really scared," Shaw quipped, and several of his men snickered or chuckled.

Davy was glad they did. It gave him some idea of where they were concealed. One was in a cluster of weeds not twenty paces from the hole.

"Give up now and I'll go easy on you," Shaw

said. "I give you my word that your deaths will be quick and painless."

A wide willow shielded the leader. Davy sighted on it, wishing the killer would poke his head out. "Only a fool takes the word of someone who has no honor," he hollered. "You'll stake us out and torture us until you're bored."

"Don't think I wouldn't like to," Shaw confessed. "But with the Sioux after our scalps, we can't linger." He paused. "Tell you what. Just hand over the women and we'll go our merry way. What do you say?"

It was Davy's turn to laugh. The abrupt change of heart was as fake as counterfeit money. "Sure," he said. "And while we're at it, we'll hand over our rifles and pistols just so you'll know we won't shoot you in the back as you walk off."

Shaw sighed. "All right. Enough of this nonsense. Flush them out, boys. Just be careful of the women."

On all sides, rifles and pistols blasted. Davy bent low as balls whizzed overhead or smacked into the wall on either side. The louder retorts of five rifles were easy to tell from those of three pistols.

That stumped Davy. Flavius had thrown every last gun into the river. The only explanation he could think of was that the slavers had extra rifles and pistols stashed in their packs and bedrolls. He should have thought of that before and had Flavius check.

The firing died down. Flavius was on his knees next to an exposed root nearly as thick as his head. It jutted a good foot into the air, shielding his right side. "We've played right into their hands," he whispered. "We're sitting ducks if we stay here."

"We'd be no better off out there," Davy said. To bolster his friend's spirits and show the cutthroat that they had a fight on their hands, he aimed at the middle of the weed patch and fired.

A man squalled like an infant and the weeds shook violently as if in a gale. "I'm hit! I'm hit! Help me, Shaw!"

"Clem, is that you?" the leader responded. "Where did they get you?"

"In the leg! I'm bleeding like a stuck pig!"

"Is that all? If you didn't take one in the vitals, you'll live. Quit your bellyaching."

"But I *hurt!*"

"You'll hurt worse if you don't shut up."

Davy took advantage of the situation, shouting, "Is that how you always treat your men, Shaw? You don't give a damn about them. All you care about is the money you'll get for the Oglalas."

Shaw was not ruffled in the least. "Nice try, Crockett, but you can't turn my boys against me. They know I treat them fairly. We all get equal shares, we all take equal risks. That's the rule." His voice wavered, as it would if he were changing position. "You're a crafty one, Tennessean, but luck is on our side."

"You think so?" Davy baited him.

"I know so." Shaw chortled. "Those canoes you had the women push into the current drifted into shore instead of away from it. And your horses came waltzing back right after you left."

Davy had one last ploy to try. "You should use those canoes and the horses to light a shuck while you still can. It won't be long before Black Buffalo and the Sioux arrive."

"Never give up, do you?" Shaw asked. "The Sioux won't get here until tomorrow afternoon, if then. We've plenty of time to finish you and your friend off."

A rifle shattered the stillness, the signal for all

the slavers to fire. Balls seemed to fly as thick as bees for several seconds. One punched into the soil an inch from Davy's elbow.

Flavius flattened when the root next to him was shattered. Flying slivers stung his cheeks and jaw, drawing blood. Outraged, he popped up and shot at what he took to be a moving shadow. Either it was his imagination or he missed, because there was no outcry.

Once more the firing ceased. Davy reloaded swiftly, expecting a concerted rush at any moment. None came, though, and after a while he realized they must have something else in mind. But what?

One of the Oglalas was holding her upper arm, a dark stain seeping from under her fingers. Davy beckoned and Eagle Woman brought her over. A ball had creased her biceps, digging a shallow furrow. She would be in a pain a spell, but she would heal.

"Tennessean!" Garth Shaw shouted. "Are you and the human pumpkin still with us?"

"We're still in the land of the living," Davy confirmed. "All you did was waste ammunition."

"We've plenty to spare," Shaw said.

Davy assumed that was a cue for the rest to shoot, but no hail of lead ensued. Not right away, and not later, either. Tense hours passed uneventfully. It was past ten clock when a tiny fire blazed to life over by the Missouri River.

"See that?" Garth Shaw shouted. He had changed position yet again. "Kline is fixing us some coffee. We'll be nice and warm out here while you shiver and go hungry. Why put yourself through all this aggravation? Those squaws aren't worth it."

"That depends on how a man sees things," Davy

David Thompson

said. "To my way of thinking, every life is precious." He thought of the ideals his father had fought for during the Revolution. "Thomas Jefferson once wrote that we all have the right to life, liberty, and the pursuit of happiness. I reckon those values are worth fighting for."

Mirth broke out on all sides.

"Oh, Lordy! Thomas Jefferson!" a man guffawed. "We have us a regular patriot here, boys!"

"And here we figured he wanted them squaws for himself!" chimed in another.

Shaw's reply was scathing. "I took you for a smart one, Tennessee, but I was wrong. Jefferson wrote those words about *white* folks, not red heathens. You can't really think they rate the same treatment as us, do you?"

Davy had never given the issue much thought, but now that he did, the answer was "Yes, I do." Shaw had no comment. Davy changed position himself in case they had it pegged. Making himself as comfortable as he could, he waited for an attack that never came. Midnight did, then two o'clock and four o'clock.

Flavius could not understand what the slavers were waiting for. The tension was practically unbearable. He fidgeted. He shifted his weight from foot to foot. Like Davy, he scanned the forest again and again.

The first pink flush of dawn tinged the eastern horizon when Davy peeked over the edge for the umpteenth time. He saw the same trees, the same bushes that were always there. Then, as he started to hunker, he noticed something strange, a bush about six feet away that had not been there the last time he looked.

Insight seared Davy like a carving knife. The cutthroats had been waiting for daylight all along!

162

They had all probably crawled as close as they could get and were awaiting the command to pounce. "Flavius—" Davy began. His warning was drowned out by a roar from Garth Shaw.

"*Now*, boys! At 'em, and the Devil take the hindmost!"

The "bush" sprang erect, the half-breed who had held it throwing it aside as he sped toward the hole. Three other bushes sprouted legs and converged, while from behind trees appeared cutthroats leveling rifles and pistols.

Flavius saw Grist and stroked his trigger. His ball caught the man high in the shoulder, spinning him around. Flavius brought his pistol up just as a heavy form hurtled over the side and slammed him to the turf. Disoriented, he was barely aware that a knife was arcing at his neck. The blast of a flintlock jolted him out of his daze.

Eagle Woman had thrust the flintlock Flavius had lent her into the killer's face and fired. The ball cored a new nostril, flipping Kline backward.

At the same time, Davy had brought up Liz. He got off his shot just as the half-breed leaped. The man's jugular burst in a gory crimson spray, spattering Davy as he sidestepped the falling body and grasped his tomahawk.

Over the rim came the other 'breed. Cuchillo, Flavius had called him. Behind Cuchillo were Shaw and Gallows and the rest, spaced out to present more difficult targets.

Davy knew that there was no stopping them, that the killers would swarm over Flavius and him, that no matter how fiercely he fought, the women were doomed to be carted off. But he did not give in.

Not for nothing were the Appalachian backwoodsmen of Tennessee widely regarded as fierce fighters. Davy's father and grandfather had both done more than their share. Now he lived up to the family heritage by whipping out his tomahawk and confronting Cuchillo as the man landed lightly and flashed a long knife at his neck.

Davy parried, swung, and was blocked in turn. He pivoted to evade a wicked thrust at his groin, then swung a blow that would have taken Cuchillo's head off had it connected.

Above and around the hole mayhem reigned. Guns boomed. Men screamed. Screams mixed with whizzing sounds. Screams punctuated by thuds.

Cuchillo speared his blade at Davy's chest. Davy twisted, felt searing pain as the knife glanced off his ribs. Spinning in a complete circle, he brought the tomahawk up and around, cleaving it into Cuchillo below the shoulder. Cuchillo buckled but gamely attempted to stab Davy in the stomach. A bound to the right took Davy in the clear. Hiking the tomahawk, he brought it swishing down onto the back of Cuchillo's neck. Spine and flesh were sheared like so much pulp.

Turning, Davy glanced up, braced for another attacker. But the battle was over. Littering the ground were the arrow-studded bodies of Garth Shaw and each and every one of his men. No body had fewer than five shafts in it. Most, like Gallows's, bristled like porcupines with eight or nine.

Black Buffalo and his warriors ringed the hole three deep. Struck-By-Blackfeet glared at Davy and brought up his bow, only to have it batted down by White-Hollow-Horn. Snapping at the younger warrior, Struck-By-Blackfeet again raised his bow. This time he was stopped by Black Buffalo himself.

The Teton leader ignored Davy and Flavius, but

questioned Eagle Woman at length. Whatever she said made an impression. He said something to Struck-By-Blackfeet that caused the hothead to flush scarlet and stomp off like an indignant bull. Finally the chief faced Davy, his hands flowing.

"I am told that our sisters owe their lives to you and your friend. For that I am grateful. But I cannot overlook that you struck a Teton warrior. He has the right to kill you if he wishes, and only my request that he spare you has stopped him."

Davy raised his hands to reply, but he was not given the opportunity.

"Struck-By-Blackfeet and those who take his side do not have to heed me. They might change their minds. My advice to you, Tail Hat, is to leave. Now. Do not speak. Do not even look at Struck-By-Blackfeet." The chief pointed toward the Missouri. "Your horses are close to the river. Take them and go. Ride as fast as you can and maybe you will live. That is the gift I give you for saving these women."

And that was exactly what Davy did. Twice Flavius tried to speak but Davy shushed him. The Sioux parted to permit them to pass. The horses were right where Black Buffalo had said they would be.

As Davy crossed the Missouri, he looked back. White-Hollow-Horn stood watching. Davy smiled and waved, and the young warrior did likewise.

"Do you mind telling me what that was all about?" Flavius inquired as their mounts stepped onto the east shore. "All that finger wriggling has me more confused than a pagan at a Baptist service."

"As soon as we're safe," Davy promised. Lashing his reins, he winked and said, "For now, ride like hell for home."

"Home?" Flavius repeated, the word conjuring fond images of his hunting hounds, the cabin he had built with his own hands, and his wife, in that order. "Why didn't you say so?" he said, beaming.

Side by side, the two Tennesseans galloped across the sprawling plain and were soon lost in the morning haze.

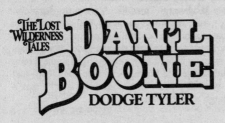

CHEYENNE

JUDD COLE

Cheyenne #19: Bloody Bones Canyon. Born the son of a great chieftain, raised by frontier settlers, Touch the Sky returns to protect his tribe. Only he can defend them from the renegades that threaten to take over the camp. But when his people need him most, the mighty warrior is forced by Cheyenne law to leave them to avenge a crime that defies all belief—the brutal slaughter of their beloved peace chief, Gray Thunder. Even Touch the Sky cannot fight two battles at once, and without his powerful magic his people will be doomed.

_4077-8 $3.99 US/$4.99 CAN

Cheyenne #11: Spirit Path. Trained as a shaman, Touch the Sky uses strong magic time and again to save the tribe. Still, the warrior is feared and distrusted as a spy for the white men who raised him. Then a rival accuses Touch the Sky of bad medicine, and if he can't prove the claim false, he'll come to a brutal end—and the Cheyenne will face utter destruction.

_3656-8 $3.99 US/$4.99 CAN

Dorchester Publishing Co., Inc.
65 Commerce Road
Stamford, CT 06902

Please add $1.75 for shipping and handling for the first book and $.50 for each book thereafter. NY, NYC, PA and CT residents, please add appropriate sales tax. No cash, stamps, or C.O.D.s. All orders shipped within 6 weeks via postal service book rate. Canadian orders require $2.00 extra postage and must be paid in U.S. dollars through a U.S. banking facility.

Name _____
Address _____
City _____ State _____ Zip _____
I have enclosed $_____ in payment for the checked book(s).
Payment <u>must</u> accompany all orders.☐ Please send a free catalog.

CHEYENNE GIANT EDITION:

BLOOD ON THE ARROWS

JUDD COLE

Follow the adventures of Touch the Sky, as he searches for a world he can call his own—in a Giant Special Edition!

Born the son of a Cheyenne warrior, raised by frontier settlers, Touch the Sky returns to his tribe and learns the ways of a mighty shaman. Then the young brave's most hated foe is brutally slain, and he stands accused of the crime. If he can't prove his innocence, he'll face the wrath of his entire people—and the hatred of the woman he loves.

_3839-0 $5.99 US/$7.99 CAN

CHEYENNE

JUDD COLE

Follow the adventures of Touch the Sky as he searches for a world he can call his own!

#3: Renegade Justice. When his adopted white parents fall victim to a gang of ruthless outlaws, Touch the Sky swears to save them—even if it means losing the trust he has risked his life to win from the Cheyenne.
__3385-2 $3.50 US/$4.50 CAN

#4: Vision Quest. While seeking a mystical sign from the Great Spirit, Touch the Sky is relentlessly pursued by his enemies. But the young brave will battle any peril that stands between him and the vision of his destiny.
__3411-5 $3.50 US/$4.50 CAN

CHEYENNE

JUDD COLE

Don't miss the adventures of Touch the Sky, as he searches for a world he can call his own.

Cheyenne #14: Death Camp. When his tribe is threatened by an outbreak of deadly disease, Touch the Sky must race against time and murderous foes. But soon, he realizes he must either forsake his heritage and trust white man's medicine—or prove his loyalty even as he watches his people die.

_3800-5 $3.99 US/$4.99 CAN

Cheyenne #15: Renegade Nation. When Touch the Sky's enemies join forces against all his people—both Indian and white—they test his warrior and shaman skills to the limit. If the fearless brave isn't strong enough, he will be powerless to stop the utter annihilation of the two worlds he loves.

_3891-9 $3.99 US/$4.99 CAN

WHITE APACHE

Jake McMasters

Follow the action-packed adventures of Clay Taggart, as he fights for revenge against settlers, soldiers, and savages.

#7: Blood Bounty. The settlers believe Clay Taggart is a ruthless desperado with neither conscience nor soul. But Taggart is just an innocent man who has a price on his head. With a motley band of Apaches, he roams the vast Southwest, waiting for the day he can clear his name—or his luck runs out and his scalp is traded for gold.

__3790-4 $3.99 US/$4.99 CAN

#8: The Trackers. In the blazing Arizona desert, a wanted man can end up as food for the buzzards. But since Clay Taggart doesn't live like a coward, he and his band of renegade Indians spend many a day feeding ruthless bushwhackers to the wolves. Then a bloodthirsty trio comes after the White Apache and his gang. But try as they might to run Taggart to the ground, he will never let anyone kill him like a dog.

__3830-7 $3.99 US/$4.99 CAN

Dorchester Publishing Co., Inc.
65 Commerce Road
Stamford, CT 06902

Please add $1.75 for shipping and handling for the first book and $.50 for each book thereafter. NY, NYC, PA and CT residents, please add appropriate sales tax. No cash, stamps, or C.O.D.s. All orders shipped within 6 weeks via postal service book rate. Canadian orders require $2.00 extra postage and must be paid in U.S. dollars through a U.S. banking facility.

Name _____

Address _____

City _____ State _____ Zip _____

I have enclosed $_____in payment for the checked book(s). Payment <u>must</u> accompany all orders.☐ Please send a free catalog.

 **Jake McMasters**

Follow the action-packed adventures of Clay Taggart, as he fights for revenge against soldiers, settlers, and savages.

#9: *Desert Fury*. From the canyons of the Arizona Territory to the deserts of Mexico, Clay Taggart and a motley crew of Apaches blaze a trail of death and vengeance. But for every bounty hunter they shoot down, another is riding hell for leather to collect the prize on their heads. And when the territorial governor offers Taggart a chance to clear his name, the deadliest tracker in the West sets his sights on the White Apache—and prepares to blast him to hell.

_3871-4 $3.99 US/$4.99 CAN

#10: *Hanged!* Although Clay Taggart has been strung up and left to rot under the burning desert sun, he isn't about to play dead. After a desperate band of Indians rescues Taggart, he heads into the Arizona wilderness and plots his revenge. One by one, Taggart hunts down his enemies, and with the help of renegade Apaches, he acts as judge, jury, and executioner. But when Taggart sets his sights on a corrupt marshal, he finds that the long arm of the law might just have more muscle than he expects.

_3899-4 $3.99 US/$4.99 CAN